The CATS
of Sanctuary Hou

The CATS

of Sanctuary House

Sister Mary Winifred

WILLOW CREEK PRESS

Published by Willow Creek Press, P.O. Box 147, Minocqua, Wisconsin 54548

Editor: Andrea Donner
Design: Amy Kolberg

Library of Congress Cataloging-in-Publication Data

Winifred, Mary, 1949-
    The cats of Sanctuary House / Sister Mary Winifred.
        p. cm.
    ISBN 1-59543-155-1 (hardcover : alk. paper)
    1. Feral cats-Maryland–Upper Fairmount–Biography. 2. Sanctuary House
(Upper Fairmount, Md.) I. Title.
    SF450.W56 2005
    636.8'009752'23–dc22
                                                    2005011638

Printed in Canada

Contents

For Annie,
who understood that some stories can never be told;
and

Dr. Edward P. Coulston,
without whose generous professional help and support,
there would be far fewer stories to tell.

Acknowledgments

Our most grateful thanks go to our primary veterinarian, Dr. Edward P. Coulston, and the staff at the Animal Clinic of Talbot, Easton, Maryland—Susan Coulston, Judy L. Wells, and Audrey Barker. We also want to thank our emergency veterinarians, Dr. Daryl Layfield-Insley and Dr. Carol R. Lewis, and the staff at Layfield Veterinary Services, Princess Anne, Maryland; and the other veterinarians who have taken care of us, Dr. William N. Spofford and Dr. Cynthia L. Gosser at Bayside Animal Hospital, Cambridge, Maryland; Dr. Linda Ferraro at St. Michaels Veterinary Clinic, St. Michaels, Maryland; and Dr. John Wilson at Brewster Veterinary Hospital, Brewster, New York. We also want to thank those many individuals who help to make Sanctuary House a safe haven.

Some of the cats at Sanctuary House have been preceded into the next life by their beloved people, whose care and love made life on earth a wonderful adventure—we will always remember them: Annie's Ron Cummings, Blossom's Helen Mace, and Ragu's Zelda Clennan.

We also thank Willow Creek Press, Andrea Donner and Amy Kolberg for making our stories into a book.

Photograph credits: Early photograph of "Thomas" and "Augusta," anonymous; "Sebastian," Karen Schaffer.

Foreword

You may wonder why a veterinarian who specializes in horses should be writing a foreword to a book about cats. One of the reasons is that my mother and the mother of Sister Mary Winifred grew up together in Texas and, in spite of time and the great Atlantic Ocean, have remained life-long friends. Through the years our families have exchanged visits and now another generation continues the friendship.

Cats are survivors and in many cases, they survive against tremendous odds. They make full use of their nine lives. They have replaced the dog as the favorite pet in the United Kingdom and hardly a day goes by that there is not mention in the newspapers of the exploits of these formidable felines.

Cats hold pride of place in the affections of people worldwide and these touching and humorous stories of these intrepid cats should have universal appeal.

D.K. Mason, BVMS MRCVS
Veterinary Surgeon
Glasgow, Scotland, United Kingdom

Introduction

The sparrow has found her a house and the swallow a nest where she may lay her young; by the side of your altars, O Lord of hosts, my King and my God. Happy are they who dwell in your house! They will always be praising you.
Psalm 84:2-3

The original Sanctuary House began with two cats, Thomas and Augusta, four parakeets, and a dream. I had come to the Eastern Shore of Maryland from the Community of the Holy Spirit in New York, hoping to establish a new Episcopal Religious Order, the Community of the Ascension, and to work with women who had been incarcerated, and their children. I taught GED classes at the local detention center and welcomed several women into our home—the latter was a rather unsuccessful effort.

But by then, there was a third cat, Theo, and a dog, Molly. Following a long-time love, I became a licensed wildlife rehabilitator, specializing in song birds and waterfowl. The ministry of Sanctuary House turned gradually, but directly, toward work not only with orphaned and injured wildlife, but with domestic animals as well.

Today, Sanctuary House at Muddy Paw in Upper Fairmount, Somerset County, Maryland, is a center for licensed wildlife rescue and rehabilitation, and home to the Community of the Ascension, and many domestic animals. The wild animals, of course, are temporary residents. The other animals are home, and while an occasional animal may be adopted, most of them will stay right here. Eight dogs and more than 40 cats live at Sanctuary House, as well as two goats, a horse, and many birds: ducks, geese, Guineas, chickens, finches, love birds, cockatiels, parakeets, and a cherry headed conure. Unlike typical convents, with a definite daily schedule, the Sanctuary House timetable is adjusted each season, and flows with the needs of the resident animals who are individually and collectively mission, avocation, and gifts from God. Some of the animals have found us on their own; some have been brought to us by friends; several of the animals have been loved by people who have gone on ahead of them to larger life; some have never been loved at all; some of them have been abused. But all of them have brought joy and life and love to Sanctuary House, and all of them have stories to tell.

These are the cats' stories just as I have learned them.

Abbie

a story for Daryl

The first time I saw calico Abbie she was sitting near the fence of our cat courtyard. The cats inside the courtyard watched her through the fence slats, and I went around to see why they were staring. As I walked near her she quickly bounded to the house across the street, and I assumed that is where she lived. I didn't see her again until the weekend.

I came home from work the next Saturday to find Callie, our old Arabian horse, leaning over the fence, looking toward the garage-barn. "Oh, Callie, I know it's dinner time," I remarked, but then noticed that she was staring at the ground. And there, sitting on the concrete walk into the barn, was Abbie. At first I thought she must have been hit by a car—her lower jaw was hanging down and she had a bloody scrape on her side. I moved cautiously, not wanting to startle her, but when I opened the barn door, she ran inside, and actually caught an unsuspecting mouse! Abbie was horribly thin, and with her injuries, could not eat or even kill the mouse—the mouse escaped into a bale of hay, and Abbie turned to look at me. I picked her up and put her into a cat carrier. She didn't resist at all, only cried softly.

I offered food and water, but Abbie only stared at it, unable to get anything into her mouth. Her bottom jaw was gray, stinking, hanging on by a rotting string of skin.

I knew that our regular veterinarian was out of town. I called several vets—Saturday evening is not an easy time to reach any doctor, but I did find one local veterinarian at home. "Probably this is just a euthanasia case," I warned him. "She's in pretty bad shape."

My neighbor, Sue, rode with us to the veterinary clinic. Whether from pain or hunger, Abbie cried softly most of the way.

The doctor took a quick look at Abbie. "I think we can fix this," he said softly. He called to his assistant who was in the barn with the horses, and Sue and I watched as he eased Abbie into sleep and deftly removed most of her lower jaw, leaving only the very back teeth on each side. "She'll be able to eat," he said. "She'll just have a serious overbite!"

He examined her other injuries and concluded that she had not been hit by a car, but had been shot by a pellet gun. Blood tests were negative for feline leukemia and AIDS. X-rays revealed no internal injuries under her shoulder lacerations.

"What about kittens," I asked, well aware that unspayed cats do not survive long outdoors without becoming pregnant.

"I didn't x-ray that far back," the vet admitted. "Let's just see how she does overnight. Call me between nine and eleven tomorrow morning."

I sang with the church choir for the nine A.M. service, my mind half on Abbie. When I reached the vet a short time later, he sounded thrilled. "Abbie is great!

She's walking around and already eating. This couldn't be better," he concluded.

On Monday, Abbie came home. She healed quickly, and soon graduated from soupy canned cat food to dry kibbles. A few weeks later, based on her rapid weight gain and extremely affectionate demeanor, my thoughts were confirmed: Abbie was indeed pregnant.

Abbie was a contented, easy-going cat, and I thought she must have been pregnant before. She ate and rested as though she knew exactly what was coming. The gray, brown and white splotches of her coat stretched and expanded as we counted the weeks.

Abbie seemed totally unconcerned, but when the kittens' due date came and passed, I began to worry. After all, Abbie had been through a lot—not only had she been shot, but the anesthesia and surgery on her jaw might well have injured the kittens. The idea of a false pregnancy was put to rest when the vet felt tiny kitten heads through Abbie's distended uterus.

Then, early one morning, just a day before we

thought she might have to Caesarean delivery, six beautiful kittens were born: first, a calico with tiger stripes; then a tiger-striped, brilliant orange kitten; next a small gray kitten with an orange mark on her head exactly like Abbie's; then two almost identical tiger-striped, gray kittens; and finally a very tiny gray kitten with white paws and a white blaze on his face. Abbie was exhausted and bled profusely after the last kitten was born.

The kittens were voraciously hungry, and Abbie dutifully lay on her side for them. She washed and attended them, but would not eat, and continued to bleed. Sadly, the tiny gray-and-white kitten died. Abbie looked at him and licked his face as I lifted him out of the box. She seemed despondent and depressed, letting the kittens eat, but not willing to eat for herself. I was afraid that Abbie might still be carrying a kitten, and also knew she had to eat in order to feed the kittens. We made a quick trip to the vet, who gave Abbie a shot and assured me that there were no more kittens. He looked at the five healthy kittens—so differently colored. "And who is your father?" he laughed.

Actually, I had a very good idea who the father was, but that is another story.

Alistair
(2000-2003)

The young tabby tom-cat, left ear torn in a recent scuffle and blue-green eyes squinted shut against the sun, walked boldly down the driveway. His tabby markings were perfectly symmetrical, as if they had been painted on with great care.

For an outdoor, feral cat he was amazingly friendly. I picked him up. "Take me in," he seemed to say.

"We do need a cat named Alistair," Sister Harriet said, "for Alistair in the British comedy *As Time Goes By.*"

"Well, okay, he can be Alistair," I replied.

After a visit to our vet to be neutered and vacci-nated, Alistair was tentatively introduced to his new brother and sister cats. He was shy with some, and very taken with others, but showed no inclination to fight. He was calm and easy going. He had known how to mark his territory and, I suppose happily for him, his surgery hadn't limited his ability. Our screened porch became his castle.

When we moved to our new home with an enclosed cat courtyard, Alistair was glad to be in the semi-outdoors again. He watched the distant birds and ignored the sounds of dogs and traffic. Alistair—or Al as he preferred to be called—was a peaceful, quiet cat. He occasionally pretended to be a lap cat, but most often he lay stretched out in a shady spot, surveying his domain. Sometimes he played with Caroline and Lucie and Leo. They chased each other in circles and then collapsed altogether in a heap.

The cats have a house, but except in very cold or wet weather, Alistair stayed outside as much as possible—no comfy cushions or "people" chairs for him! And he was healthy—no fleas, no ear mites, no allergies, or rotten teeth. Alistair was a "no problem" cat.

Alistair also loved breakfast! All of the cats run to me in the morning, but Al seemed especially delighted with mornings. "I've been waiting all night for you," he seemed to say. He always yawned, stretched, and looked up at me.

One sunny autumn morning, I was startled not to see him. Because it had been raining the night before, I had shut the cat house doors, leaving only the small cat door open.

"Maybe he's inside," I said to the other cats, although that seemed unlikely, and they only stared blankly at me. "Al," I called, "Alistair."

Sasha and Gracie, who often stay inside the cat house, were sitting outside. Other cats walked around my feet, purring for breakfast. "Al," I called again as I walked toward the cat house.

I opened the doors, and there he was—dead.

Theo, a large orange cat, sat nearby, as if he were keeping watch. Al was lying beside a small dish of cat food—there seemed to have been no long suffering.

Mercifully, Al had apparently died as quietly and peacefully as he had lived.

"Probably cardiomyopathy," the vet concluded. "It can be extremely painful or very quick with no warning signs."

My nephew, Norman, helped me bury Al's body. His spirit, I'll wager, is off discovering his new territory and domain.

[This story was first published in *Cats & Kittens* magazine in March 2005.]

Augusta
(1986-2003)

I heard the meow as I was taking the garbage outside. It was a plaintive sound and came from the high weeds behind the dumpster. I stopped and listened, as the meows gradually grew closer. I sat down on the concrete curb and said "meow" in return. And then slowly, out of the weeds, stepped a very thin gray cat. She was starvingly thin, and walked with a slight limp.

I gathered her into my arms and carried her inside. She ate and drank, then ate some more, before falling asleep. In the morning I took her to our veterinarian. All of her tests were negative and she had been spayed. "But she is starving," the vet warned. "You need to feed her small amounts often. You'll have to keep an eye on her."

At home I already had a cat named Thomas, after an Archbishop of Canterbury. The new cat was named Augusta, after St. Augustine of Canterbury, and soon we began calling her Gussie.

Thomas was my first cat and I had assumed—incorrectly—that Thomas and Gussie would be immediate friends. Instead they circled each other, making soft, guttural, growling sounds. I pleaded, cajoled, begged, and threatened, but neither would go near the other. By night time, I had tried all of my ideas.

"Okay, you two," I said to the cats, "this is a big house. You just figure out how to get along." I shut the door to my bedroom and turned off the light.

The next morning, I opened the door and stepped into the hallway. Thomas and Gussie came walking toward me, rubbing against each other, tails held high.

"Excellent!" I greeted them.

Gussie grew strong and healthy, and she and Thomas became fast friends. Thomas was always a very relaxed, happy-go-lucky cat, and there were many things about catdom that he had neglected to tell me! It was, therefore, left to Gussie to teach me many things about cats, such as: some cats do not like to have their claws trimmed; cats do not always use the litter box; cats do not have to explain why they are not using the litter box; some cats do not eat food that is not "cat food."

Some cats do not walk willingly into cat carriers; some cats get very car sick and can throw up through the bars of a cat carrier onto the car seat; some cats do not catch mice and then let them escape unharmed.

Over the years, there were many other things that Gussie taught me, too—how to go on with life when you lose the friend you love the most; how to be graceful and accepting of illness and pain; how to love unconditionally.

After Thomas died in 2001, Gussie began coming to chapel for Morning and Evening Prayer. She came when she heard the bell and always sat in the same chair. Sometimes it looked as if she were asleep, but I imagine she was praying her own cat prayers.

Gussie died in 2003, two years after her beloved Thomas and following a long bout with mammary cancer. She was, we calculated, about 17 years old. She was a wise and good cat. I miss her, and still sometimes look around to see if she is on her special chair. In heart and mind, Gussie is very much here with me.

Beulah, Rufus, Tovia, Gloria, & Linus

The five kittens of Abbie and Thomas II, in birth order, are calico Beulah, called Buttons; bright orange Rufus; Tovia, who has her mother's muted colors and markings; Gloria, gray with a hint of muted calico colors; and Linus, who now grown up, looks so much like Thomas II that they are often mistaken for each other.

Whether or not birth order is a valid indicator of

personality, these five young cats have distinct attitudes toward life. Of course, they played together when they were very young and were excellently cared for and taught by Abbie. Abbie was a strict and loving mother. She was extremely affectionate and protective of her kittens. She allowed them to climb on her, lick her face, and pull her tail. She kept them clean and called them to her when they ventured away. She taught them to use the litter box and insisted that they play nicely with each other.

But when the kittens were five weeks old and eating on their own, she kissed them good-bye and moved to the cat courtyard. "I've given you a good start in life," she seemed to say, "now you're on your own!"

The kittens apparently accepted this arrangement quite happily. There was no sibling rivalry and all five of the kittens like other cats. As the months went by, the three girls were moved to one room and the two boys to another. Rufus and Linus met their father for the first time, and he willingly accepted them, calmly tolerating their young cat antics and energy.

When the girls were old enough to be spayed, they moved to the cat courtyard. Abbie was glad to see them, and quietly let them know that in the courtyard she was the alpha cat.

Beulah, whose name means "beautiful" and "peace," had earlier told me to call her Buttons. She ran into the sunshine of the courtyard without a look back. She was immediately welcomed by all of the other cats, and was thrilled to discover a world of practice golf balls and fluttering leaves. She is independent and self-assured—a true calico in heart and mind!

Tovia, whose name means "good one," is very much a good one. She, too, happily joined the courtyard family, but she likes to be cuddled and held, and always runs to me. She is sweet and gentle, and adores Katie, the ancient beagle who sometimes visits the courtyard.

Gloria also dashed into the courtyard—amazed at how much space she had suddenly inherited. As the most energetic of the kittens, she was also the first to get in dangerous trouble: she discovered how to get to the top of the fence! No cat before or since has done that. Fortunately, I found her. She was trying unsuccessfully to get back into the courtyard. My heart was racing as I lifted her back to safety and held her close. "Never, ever do that again, Gloria," I warned. "You could get lost." And then I explained to her that she would have to live in the house until she was too old or too fat to leap to the top of the fence. I think she understood that I was afraid for her—she has quite contentedly transitioned back to a full-time house cat!

Two months later the boys were ready to follow their sisters to the courtyard.

Rufus, the smaller of the two, and the one who has the same smiling expression as Buttons, went out first. He was a little shy, but Tovia rushed up to him and began licking his head and rubbing against him. With such a warm sibling welcome he soon felt right at home.

Linus, like Buttons, is independent and was excited to find courtyard toys and friends. Occasionally, Linus slips back into the house for a special cat food treat breakfast, but he is always eager to go back where he can watch the wide sky and play tag with the other cats.

What blessings Abbie, Thomas II, and their kittens have brought to all of us!

Blossom

a story for Deanna

$\mathcal{M}$y friend, Deanna, called to say that her elderly neighbor, Miss Helen had died. "So, you know Miss Helen had pets," she continued.

"What pets?" I asked, knowing exactly where the conversation was heading.

"Well, a love bird—her daughter-in-law is taking the bird. And her dog, Dally, is going to live with me. But, then there's Blossom."

"Blossom?" I questioned. "And would Blossom be a cat?"

"Exactly," Deanna answered. She sounded glad that I had said the word "cat."

"Okay," I agreed, "after all, I did once promise to

help Miss Helen. But I can only take Blossom if she is healthy and up to date on her shots. I can't put my other cats at risk."

We agreed to relay Blossom—Deanna would take her to the vet for tests and shots, and, all being well, I would pick her up and bring her home. In my heart, I doubted that Blossom was healthy. Although she had been spayed at an early age, she had basically been an outside cat for many years. Blossom was smart; every-day she walked side by side with Miss Helen's dog in order to go inside for dinner and hugs—but then she was put back outside. She had eaten well, and was friendly with people and dogs, but she was not up to date on any shots.

I called the vet to check on her.

"She's good to go!" the vet replied. "She does have an upper respiratory condition, but that may be chronic at this point; we'll try antibiotics. She is an old cat—at least fifteen"

I took Blossom and a month's supply of antibiotics. Blossom was a small, very muscular orange-and–white cat; she had a marked head tilt and a distinct, soft, meow voice. We became friends immediately.

For a cat who had spent much of her life outdoors, Blossom has adjusted quickly and happily to a sedate indoor routine. I did take her to visit our cat courtyard, but she wrapped her front legs around my neck. "I think I'll just stay in," she seemed to say.

Blossom stayed in my bedroom and claimed my pillow as her own. At first, no other cats were even allowed on the bed. Blossom never did anything to them—she only looked at them with her slightly crooked stare and they backed down. "She's a tyrant," I remarked to the vet.

Blossom never ate directly from a dish. She pushed the food onto the floor and then gingerly picked it up with her front paw, looked at it, and then ate. "Really messy," I complained to the vet.

"Survival techniques," he explained. "She didn't get this old living outside without being very clever and very careful."

Little by little, Blossom admitted the other cats into

her circle of friends. They curl up together for naps and sit close together to gaze out of the window at birds and stars. And sometimes, Blossom will eat food from a dish.

Now I wonder how I got along without her—my awesome, orange Blossom!

[This story was first published in *Cats & Kittens* magazine in September 2004.]

Caroline
a story for Cyn

Of I ever doubted that there is communication between people and animals, a tiny orange and gray kitten laid those doubts to rest.

In fact, I might have missed the kitten altogether, except for the intervention of our other cats. There they sat—staring intently out of the front window.

"Lucie," I said, "Sasha, Patrick." They continued in their sphinx-like trance, concentrating only on the window in front of them. I suspected that they were watching a bird, or even a piece of paper fluttering down the sidewalk. But not wanting to be left out of their game, I too went to the window.

And there she was. A tiny ball of orange and gray

fur, staring up at the windows, her huge yellow eyes returning the gazes from inside.

"Well, no, we can't just leave her there," I said to any cat who would listen. I walked outside and scooped her up in one hand. She was tame, perfectly gentle. She snuggled close to my chest and began to purr. She smelled like summer flowers.

"You're not a homeless kitty," I told her. "Somebody must really be missing you!"

She drank a saucer of milk and fell asleep immediately—exhausted. I checked with the animal shelter and every vet in town, and scanned the newspaper "lost and found" columns for days. No one was missing an orange and gray kitten.

She gradually became part of our extended family. The older cats loved her—after all, they had "found" her. And our other kitten, Gracie, at last had someone her own size and energy level.

I had been sure we'd find her family and had purposely not given her a name. I called her "Kitten," and then "Kitty." She ignored me completely.

"Okay," I gave in, "you need a real name. How about Nell, and we can call you Nellie?"

No response.

I read lists of names to her. Bible names: Sarah, Rebecca, Joanna, Naomi; names of cats in literature and art: Inges, Meg, Priscilla; and names of T.S. Eliot cats: Jennyanydots, Griddlebone, Electra.

No, none of those.

I cradled her in my arm. I shut my eyes and listened to her purr. I felt her heart beat and my heart beat. Intently, silently, I thought: who are you?

"My name is Caroline," she thought back.

"Then Caroline it is," I said out loud.

She jumped down, determined to pounce on Gracie.

"Caroline," I called.

She turned back and gazed unblinkingly at me. And, yes, I believe she did smile!

[This story was first published in *Cats & Kittens* magazine in September 2003.]

Casey

Casey was born a few blocks away from Sanctuary House into an uncontained, un-cared-for feral cat colony. As a very young kitten, he had suffered from a severe respiratory infection; it was probably surprising that he survived at all. He was left with a chronic sinus condition that caused a wheezing sound when he breathed and purred. Sometimes there was not enough food at his home, so Casey was thin and malnourished. And, of course, he was covered with fleas.

In his first summer, when the weather was very hot and dry, Casey set out from his birth place to find a new home where food, and especially water, were always available. Happily for him, he only had to go a short distance, across the street, before he was welcomed by a neighbor. She, however, was unable to keep Casey safely indoors, and so we agreed that he would move to Sanctuary House, where he could live in the cat courtyard.

Casey walked into the courtyard as though he had always been there. From the very beginning, he was friends with everyone. Perhaps because he was young and still rather small, the older cats greeted him easily and nonthreateningly. At one side of the courtyard is a large drinking pool, and Casey was delighted to discover this constant source of cool water.

It has been a few months since Casey came to live with us. He is still very small and thin, but will probably fill out as he grows older. I suspect that, because of his nasal damage, he cannot taste food, but he watches the older cats and always runs to the food dish when I fill it.

Casey has not told me his whole story yet, but he has taught us these valuable lessons:

Be brave: go out into the world to search for what you need;

Be friendly: people and other cats will love you if you are gentle, fun and loving;

Be flexible: it's OK to try new things;

Be wise: watch the older cats and learn from them.

Little Casey watches me closely... he has no intention of becoming a house cat, but he is delighted to come in for any leftovers in Izzy's dish. Then he dashes outside again. "You're it," he calls to Zoë, Rosie, Buttons, Tovia, and Gloria.

"Just catch us if you can," the girls meow back. And they all take off on kitten adventures—leaping over older cats, knocking over a dish of food, jumping in and out of the mint, and hiding behind a rose bush.

Charley

a story for Carol

"Do you have five minutes?" my friend Sue asked. I was leaving the post office and planning to run other errands in an otherwise uncrowded afternoon.

"Five minutes? Sure, what's up?" I responded.

"Well, I think I saw an injured cat at the side of the road, just a mile or so away."

"Okay, let's go."

I followed Sue back down our country road until we found him. The scrawny adolescent was stumbling and circling around. It had been raining and he was soaking wet. I scooped him up in a towel. He had many cuts and scrapes, one eye was swollen shut, his nose was bleeding. But worst of all, he was covered with maggots—they crawled in and out of his nose and eyes, and packed his ears.

"This is not good," I said to Sue. We put him in the car and she called ahead to the vet. I had planned to let Sue take the cat, but then decided that my errands could wait.

Fortunately, it was a slow afternoon at our local veterinary hospital. Miraculously, blood tests revealed that Charley did not have any diseases, but he was nearly dead. In addition to the maggots that now crawled from every opening in his body, he was covered with fleas. He was very thin and weak.

After hours of washing away maggots, we left Charley for the night, all of us agreeing that if he lived through the night it would be a miracle. Based on his primary injuries, the vet concluded that he had been caught in the fan belt of a car. Probably he had climbed under the hood of a car to escape recent heavy rain and wind.

And so it happened that Charley is a miracle, because the next morning he was still alive! Two days later, he was able to eat on his own and was allowed to come home.

Charley is still recovering from his injuries. He lost one eye and only recently has regained much of his typical cat coordination. He is beginning to try climbing, but does not yet run or jump. He greatly enjoys playing with practice golf balls, and another small kitten, Elijah, keeps him company in the cat "infirmary."

"Some five minutes," I commented to Sue, as we watched Charley and Elijah playing.

"What do you mean?" she asked.

"Remember, you asked if I had five minutes," I reminded her. "Charley, the miracle cat, is doing so well now, I expect that you might have asked for five minutes and 20 years—at least we can hope so!"

Charley stopped chasing Elijah and looked directly at me. He winked his good eye. "I'll be here," he thought, and then turned back to resume his kitten game with Elijah.

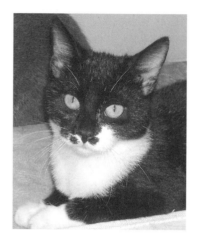

Elijah

Whether it's setting the table for a holiday feast or keeping track of cats, I usually set or save an extra place "for Elijah," following the Jewish custom of always looking for the prophet Elijah to return.

And so when my friend, Irene, asked if I rescued cats, I knew—with a house nearly full of cats—that Elijah might be coming! I might just need to use the one empty space.

Irene's granddaughter had found the tiny black and white kitten almost in the street one night. In fact, she was afraid that her car had hit him—but that was not the case. However, the kitten was injured, and had to have what remained of his tail removed. Irene's granddaughter was not able to keep the kitten, but wanted to find a safe home for him where he would be cared for and loved.

When she asked me about adopting a cat though, Irene didn't say "kitten," so I expected that I was agreeing to a full-grown cat. I immediately began thinking of introducing an adult cat to our cat court-yard. Imagine my surprise when I first met Elijah! He was a tiny kitten who fit easily into one hand. "Elijah," I whispered to him, as he stared into my face.

Because Elijah was so small and had had ringworm, I had to keep him isolated from the other cats for a few weeks. At first he was content to live by himself in the upstairs bathroom, but little by little he discovered that there was fun cat life beyond the door!

As soon as he was able to be with the other cats, Eli-jah had a special mission: he became the playmate for Charley. Charley had been horribly injured and needed a long time of rest and quiet to recover, but he certainly didn't need or want to be isolated. And so, Elijah was drafted to help. It was a role that thrilled him! Not only did he genuinely like Charley and enjoy playing with him, but he, too, now out of isolation, was delighted to discover a cat friend who was as gentle as he. The two kittens, who had suffered so much in their short lives, now had each other, and they happily shared a food dish and curled close together for cat naps.

Now, Elijah and Charley are growing up. They are healthy and getting stronger everyday. They even get into typical kitten mischief! But most of all, they are great kitten friends.

Gracie

Many of our cats are named after Archbishops of Canterbury... we call them The Canterbury Tails. Only recently, though, did we add the "Title" cat! [Note: "His Grace" or "Your Grace" is a title of courtesy for archbishops... that would make Gracie the first "Her Grace!"]

Sister Harriet put down the telephone. "It's Jack," she said. "He found a kitten in the parking lot."

"So," I stalled.

"I'll pick her up," Sister offered.

Actually, our Community usually rescues injured, wild birds. But after five years in a small town, "birds" had been transformed into "animals," and "wild"—well, that just means "homeless."

Dogs, cats, rabbits, and squirrels have joined ducks, herons, geese, swans, and countless song birds.

This leggy, gray kitten was skinny—scrawny and listless.

"A fever of unknown origin," our vet pronounced, after finding all tests negative for known feline diseases. "Just keep her warm, and try to get her to eat and drink."

I took a saucer of baby food chicken, mixed with an antibiotic, to the comforter where the kitten was curled into a ball. She looked up and staggered to her feet. Her eyes, watering and glistening from the fever, never left the plate. She ate the entire jar of baby food, hardly stopping for a breath. Then she curled up beside the plate and slept for hours.

Miraculously, when she woke up, her fever was gone. After days of rest and antibiotic-laced baby food, she was as rambunctious and bouncy as any kitten who ever lived. Her gray fur grew sleek and shiny.

She met our other cats with self-assurance and nonchalance. She was confident, dignified, even superior, and afraid of no cat.

"Oh, Gracie," I said, "Miss Grace. Grace, the Ace. You must be a Canterbury Tail, too!"

"She is," Sister Harriet said. "She's the title cat: Her Grace!"

Growltiger
and
Mabel

a story for Susan

Growltiger almost didn't make it as a cat of Sanctuary House at all. I had seen the small gray cat in the field and was concerned because he seemed very thin and raggedy. However, he was also very illusive—I only saw him at dusk or if I happened to go outside at night, when illumination from the motion detection lights showed him in the shadows. Concerned the "he" might be "she," and have kittens on the way, I set the Havahart trap.

Sure enough, the next morning the gray cat was in

the trap, and he—definitely he—was in very poor condition. His left eye was ruptured, swollen, and protruding from his skull, and he was covered with numerous scratches, fleas, and ticks. And, on top of that, he was viciously wild, hissing, spitting, and trying frantically to scratch me and get out of the trap. I expected that the vet would euthanize this cat, and consoled myself with the thought that at least that would be a more peaceful death than dying in the wild from infection or being killed by a predatory fox, hawk, or owl.

The vet agreed with me—not only was the cat in terrible physical condition, his personality and demeanor were that of a wild animal. The plan was to sedate the cat by putting a drug in his food, and then inject a lethal drug.

I left the cat at the vet's office, promising to pick up his body the next day.

However, when I returned the next morning, I learned that the cat had not touched the drugged food. He had calmed down considerably, but still hissed and growled and tried to attack through the bars of the trap if anyone got too close. But his calm demeanor when no one was nearby was his proverbial paw in the door.

"See, he's really a good cat," Susan, the vet's wife who worked as the office receptionist commented. "He was just afraid. Eddie, you could remove his bad eye and neuter him, and by the time he's well, he would probably be tame."

I looked at her skeptically—the cat was pretty wild. "Okay, we'll try it," her husband agreed.

Two hours of surgery later, we were on our way home. The cat was heavily sedated so that he would not wake up on our two hour drive, and I had another shot of medication to give him after transferring him from the cat carrier into his new crate home. The timing was perfect; he slept soundly on the trip. I gave him the shot for pain when we got home so that he would rest through the night. He would also need a month of antibiotics to ward off any infection in his eye. Happily, he was quite willing to take the medicine mixed with his food.

Because the cat has only one eye and because his method of speaking is most often a growl, I named him Growltiger after the cat in T.S. Eliot's poem in *Old Possum's Book of Practical Cats.*

In spite of Susan's prediction, Growltiger has never become truly tame. Growltiger does look at me when I speak to him, and sits passively when I reach into his large cage to clean the litter box and to give him food and water, but he will not allow me to touch him. His eye has healed completely and his whiskers, which had to be shaved off for his face surgery, have grown back. Perhaps, I decided, he would rather be outside again—I would feed him, of course, but he could live in the barn and come and go as he pleased.

I took his cage outside and opened the door. He sat, staring at me as though he were waiting for me to clean the litter box. "Go on," I said. "You're free." He didn't move at all.

Thinking that he might be overcome by seeing so much of the outdoors all at once, I carried the cage into the barn. I put food and water and a litter box where he could easily see them, and walked out, leaving the cage door open. He had not eaten breakfast, so I was certain that he would go out for food, and would then realize that he was no longer captive.

Several hours later I returned to the barn to get the cage. There he was, still sitting inside the cage. He had not gone out even to eat or drink.

And so, I brought him back inside. He lives—happily, I think—in a large crate beside two windows, and next to the dogs' night crates. It is his own little world, with special arrangements that allow him to hide or to sit on a raised shelf so that he can survey the goings-on in the house.

Then, to make Growltiger's life more complete, a companion came to live with him! Mabel is a black and white cat who was rescued by Susan from an about-to-be-demolished building. Mabel had several older kittens with her—the kittens were thrilled to become inside house pets, but Mabel is wild, a feral cat who had only lived under a house, never inside. Mabel was spayed, but after months of trying to tame her, we decided that she would come live with Growltiger. Mabel loves other cats, especially if they are far away from people.

Growltiger and Mabel immediately touched noses and butted their heads together. The very first night the two cats were together, Mabel huddled in a cat carrier inside their crate, and Growltiger lay right at the door of the carrier, his paw reaching in to comfort Mabel. At first, Mabel found the new situation somewhat frightening, but she soon began to trust her new space. And her new friend? She definitely trusts him!

Now, the two cats share a cat-bed basket and take turns surveying their world from the shelf. Another attempt to let them out into the courtyard fell flat— neither would even consider leaving their "home base."

Growltiger and I are thrilled that Mabel is here, and I think she is thrilled, too!

Henry

Most of the cats at Sanctuary House are simply domestic long hair or domestic short hair cats. There are several Maine Coon cats, and Lucie and Tut are part Siamese. When Henry moved in he was the most unusual cat to date. Henry is a Havana Brown. His brown fur is dark chocolate colored in winter, and reddish, henna brown—like a Cuban cigar—in summer. Henry has brilliant green eyes. He is one of the most affectionate cats at Sanctuary House; he loves to be held and is always ready to greet people as well as the other cats who live here with him.

But Henry's early life was not so simple! Although we knew nothing of the very first details of his life, when we met Henry he had been thrown—literally thrown—out of his home. According to a neighbor, the young cat had belonged to a woman and her boyfriend, both of whom seemed to be involved in alcohol and other drugs, although she never knew exactly what they were doing. Henry had, it seemed, managed to scratch the boyfriend, who had then thrown him from the window. Cat dishes, toys, and litter box had also been thrown into the bushes and weeds in the alley. I walked past, just as the poor cat was sniffing his empty food bowl.

I called softly, "Come here, kitty, kitty," and the thin brown cat bounded toward me.

"You can bring him back in," a foggy voice said. The boyfriend, dressed only in boxer shorts, leaned out of the first floor window. His eyes were glazed and bloodshot; he was smoking and his voice was a little slurred. "He's a mean, mean cat, a stupid cat," he continued.

"Oh no," I said. "You threw him out. I found him and now he's mine. He's going home with me." Henry cuddled against my neck. I think he understood that he was fortunate to escape!

"Whatever," the young man said as he stumbled away from the window, back into the darkness of the room.

Except for being very hungry, Henry seemed none the worse for his ordeal. He easily moved to the cat courtyard with our other cats, making friends almost immediately. He is an easy-going, easy to love cat—and he has never intentionally scratched anyone here!

"What a beautiful cat," my friend Sue remarked. "I know someone who is looking for a Havana brown. She would be willing to pay at least $200 for one."

"Well, this isn't just any Havana brown," I responded. "He's Henry, and he's not for sale—never, not for any amount of money. He's home, now, and he's staying right here."

Henry rubbed against my leg and we smiled at each other. That's my Henry!

Ida, Ada, and Dora

When Abbie's kittens began to grow up, I thought our days with kittens were over. Since we have many animals at Sanctuary House, and our cat areas seemed full, we had decided not to take additional cats. But then there was an October e-mail from the county humane society. Three very young, abandoned kittens had been discovered under the bushes in a woman's backyard. She was not able to care for the kittens, who still needed to be bottle fed, because she had a baby of her own—but she did want to take the kittens back once they were older. The humane society was looking for a foster home where the kittens could be fed until they could eat on their own. I agreed to take the kittens for a few weeks.

When I picked the kittens up, however, I was told that their original home was not safe—they would be moved to another shelter when they were old enough to eat. I think the humane society was afraid I would not take them and wanted to be sure that I knew there was a plan for the kittens.

They were in a covered box and I let them sleep until we got home. When I looked into the box, they were cuddled together—one all black kitten, one mostly black with white markings, and one mostly white with black patches. All three were girls. The mostly white one looked like a tiny Izzy. "You'll have to have a name that begins with an I," I told her.

As a Gilbert and Sullivan fan, the name that immediately came to mind was Ida, from the musical *Princess Ida*. Another character in the musical is Ada, so I named the other black and white kitten Ada. The all black kitten I called Hallie for Halloween—but the

THE CATS OF SANCTUARY HOUSE

name just didn't fit. Soon I began calling her Dora, and she seemed to know her name right away!

I kept reminding myself not to get attached to these kittens, because in a few weeks they would be going to another home. I fed them frequently during the day and even in the night. I was losing the attachment battle, but I was still fighting!

And then, Ida, the smallest of the three, got terribly sick. She was limp and would not eat. I called the vet, who reminded me that she might have an unknown disease or congenital problem—we suspected that this was a case of fading kitten syndrome. "She's probably not going to make it," he warned.

I refused to give up—if Ida did die, it wouldn't be because I hadn't tried. I put a drop of corn syrup on her tongue. She swallowed. For the next 12 hours, I fed her one drop of formula and corn syrup at a time with a tiny syringe. Gradually, she regained strength and soon she was again able to drink from the nursing bottle. I told her she was a miracle kitten.

All three kittens were gaining strength, playing

together, and beginning to eat on their own. And then came another set back. One morning when I reached into their box, Ida was again limp. She was cold to touch—in fact, I thought, at first, that she was dead. Somehow in the night she had gotten away from the warm blanket where Ada and Dora lay curled together. I picked Ida up and held her close to my heart. I massaged her and wrapped her in warm towels. She was much too cold to eat, and did not seem to be getting warmer. I rubbed her head, paws, and chest. Her eyes were open very wide, but I knew that she could not see me.

Suddenly she cried loudly and stretched her front paws up to my face. I leaned close to her and she tried frantically to suck my cheek and lips. I gave her a small drink of warm milk. She fell asleep for hours, curled into the hot towels.

When she woke up, she drank more milk and then leaned against my chest. "Get well, little Ida," I said. "You girls aren't going anywhere else—you're home now," I promised.

THE CATS OF SANCTUARY HOUSE

Ida, Ada, and Dora are growing into energetic, leggy kittens. Each has a remarkably distinct personality.

Dora is the gentlest, quietest, of the three, and always looks before stepping into a new situation.

Ada is the most affectionate. She is inquisitive, but reserved and is usually a follower.

Ida is the wildcat of the group. Although she is the smallest and most physically delicate, she dashes headlong into everything. She is a mischief maker and discoverer. Unlike Dora and Ada, she never for a minute considers danger or fear. "Good thing you have nine lives, Ida!" I often say when I catch up to her.

And then she runs off again, followed by Ada and Dora.

Inky

Onky was rescued by my friend Susan, who saw the little black kitten sitting dangerously near a car's front wheel. Actually, someone was about to move the car—the kitten, whose eyes were swollen shut because of infection, did not move. Fortunately, Susan's shout to the driver averted a disaster.

Equally fortunate, Susan's husband is a veterinarian, and with his care, the kitten was soon on the mend. During his convalescence, the kitten's normal energy level returned, and he turned into a little hellion! He routinely overturned his food and water dishes, shredded the paper in his litter box, and became an accomplished escape artist. He learned to open his cage in the clinic, and when measures were taken to secure the door, he discovered how to take advantage of his care-givers. As soon as his cage door was opened he leaped on to the shoulder or head of the staff person, and was gone—dashing around the clinic, climbing over furniture, or hiding behind a box.

Susan had originally called the kitten "Sam," but he did not really answer to that name. I started calling him "Inky" or "Inks," because of his dark color. He didn't pay much attention to those names either, at first, but "Inky" stuck, and gradually he did become Inky!

By the time he was healthy again, it was obvious that Inky was not going to be a contented cat until he had room to employ his vast energy. Susan and I compared notes—this kitten was near the same age as my Quin—perhaps they would be good playmates. I took Inky home for a weekend play date.

The two adolescents looked at each other, each seeing a true kindred spirit. They raced around the room, jumping on and off of the bed and dresser, and then collapsed together for a nap.

Although Inky was a little startled by Quin's propensity for growling and screeching, the two became instant friends. Quin tried to teach Inky to climb the door frame, a skill he never mastered; and he instructed her about shredding paper and jumping on the bare feet of unsuspecting sleepers—skills which she did indeed master!

Following Quin and Inky's successful first play date, Susan decided that Inky could move to Sanctuary House on a more permanent basis. Inky visited the cat courtyard, but perhaps because of his frightening early experiences, he prefers to stay completely inside. He still likes to play with Quin, but has found new friends, too. His current soul mates are Noah and Josie; and more often than not, those three have planned a surprise for me when I walk through the door that I cannot even imagine!

Izzy

"**A**re you sure you want to delete the e-mail program?" Fortunately I read the question before simply hitting the enter button on my computer!

Ever since Izzy has come to Sanctuary House and found his favorite day dreaming place on my desk, I have had to realize that he, too, uses my computer, and sometimes he even adds to—or erases—my words!

Most of the cats at Sanctuary House live in the cat courtyard where they have their own cat house, brick patio and large flower beds. A few cats—very old or very young ones—occupy an upstairs bedroom.

And then there is Izzy, the downstairs cat. Izzy came to us when his former owners decided to make major life changes that did not include Izzy. Izzy had been quite ill and, faced with the possibility of his continuing illness, they asked the vet to find a new home for him.

After months of careful nursing, Izzy has regained his good health. Soft white and gray fur hide a long scar on his shoulder, and happily Izzy has no signs of his earlier injuries or sickness. His left ear is missing one edge, but I imagine that injury dates to a much earlier stage in his life, even before he became a house cat!

I had thought, of course, that once healed, Izzy would move to the courtyard with the other cats. He, on the other hand, had quite different plans, and has set about finding numerous reasons and excuses for staying indoors. Izzy is adept at opening cabinet doors and drawers, and so became last winter's best mouser. He is the "watch cat," sitting patiently in the window when I am away, waiting for me to return. When I fold newly washed clothes, Izzy is there to help; when I caned a rocking chair, Izzy kept track of every strand of cane! He periodically races through the downstairs rooms and supervises the dogs and Curly, the cherry-headed Conure. On numerous occasions he has rearranged the items on the kitchen counters and on the fireplace mantle. He is part of the wake-up alarm system in the mornings, and he is the first to fall asleep watching the evening news.

I do believe that Izzy wants to learn to play chess, although I have not been able to convince him that broad paw swipes that take out many chess pieces at once are not allowed. Izzy plays chess, like everything else in life, by his own rules.

And, of course, Izzy is writing his memoirs—and helping me write mine—or perhaps he is only editing my freelance work. How, I wonder, did the house ever function before Izzy came to live with us.

Jackson

Jackson is one of the newer additions to our cat family and is a perfect example of the type of cat who lives at Sanctuary House—a much loved pet who, for whatever reason, decided that he would not use a litter box! Actually, Jackson has had several homes, but his sometimes-abrasive personality and poor litter box etiquette were the reasons that he found himself living in the courtyard at Sanctuary House.

However, that location proved not to suit him at all. He tried to bully the other cats—but the calicoes, who as a group believe they are in charge, were having none of that! The courtyard had always felt open and relaxed. With Jackson living there, it suddenly seemed cramped and tense.

We moved Jackson to an indoor cat room. With fewer cats, and a lot of play space and no furniture to ruin, we thought that he would be happier there. But, he went on a hunger strike. He didn't, it seemed, like the two older orange cats, Blossom and Solomon, nor did he appreciate the antics of the younger Inky and Josie.

We moved him again. This time, he and Zella-Judy shared the upstairs bathroom. With its window view of the fields and woods behind the house, I hoped that Jackson would be content. And he was. He immediately adopted the bathtub as his own, and only mildly objected to being moved temporarily to allow for people showers. This time, though, it was his roommate who objected. At only half Jackson's size, Zella-Judy took a long look at him and hissed. When he didn't respond, she turned with a growl and got into her sleeping box. For a few days she tolerated Jackson's presence. Every time I went into the room, she looked at him and growled. I ignored her. So, in typical cat fashion, she decided to make her feelings abundantly clear to me—she completely stopped using the litter box! I, of course, mistakenly thought it was Jackson who was not using the litter box. I fussed and scolded him—and he even looked ashamed, while all the time, Zella-Judy slept, or at least pretended to sleep!

It was time for Jackson to move again. Immediately when I took him out, Zella-Judy urinated on the floor once more—I think to impress upon me that I'd better not bring another cat into her space!

Jackson moved to my bedroom. He began to chase and hiss at Quin and Goldie. They just looked at him. "Idiot," Goldie thought. "Don't even go there," Quin thought. He looked straight at them and loudly, angrily meowed. "I wouldn't, if I were you," I said.

I think Jackson knows he has met his match! He is eating now and for the most part being friendly—and he even uses the litter box!

Jake

a story for Nola and Judy

J ake's story—Jake's life really—began in the winter, during a prolonged freeze. Ice was everywhere, on trees and road, boats and sidewalks. It was not typical Maryland weather at all! Jake and his kitten siblings were born on a boat, but their mother, no doubt looking for a warmer shelter, moved them into the woods while they were still very small.

Every day, Jake's mother, a quite wild, feral cat, left her kittens to find food at a nearby house, and then returned to feed and care for her little ones. One day, when winter was just beginning to end, the kittens followed her out of the woods to the house.

One by one, mother cat and kittens were trapped so

that they could be given needed vaccines and other medical care. The last kitten to be caught was Jake. For many years, that same house—its people and dogs— were Jake's home and family. Eventually Jake's person went to live with her daughter—in a house with many little, rescued dogs. Jake is a quiet soul, who enjoys peace and calm. Finding himself far outnumbered by dogs, especially little yappy dogs, was more than Jake had bargained for. He was glad to have his own room away from the dogs, but in his cat heart he was lonely and yearned for a cat companion.

And so, he came to stay at Sanctuary House. Now he found himself one in a large group of cats—and that was somewhat overwhelming, too. At first Jake hid in a closet and then in a desk drawer, but gradually he began to interact with the other cats. Slowly he discovered that he could play with Inky and Noah. Then, Abbie moved into the room, and Jake went back into hiding—he just was not prepared for the aggressive, calico personality!

So I moved Jake again, this time into a room with

Zella, another quiet introvert. The two cats ignored each other for a few days, and then, as if each one had suddenly recognized that another cat was in the room, they walked toward each other, tentatively touched noses, and then rubbed heads. I do believe there was a very quiet purring sound surrounding them!

The moral of this story? There is some cat for every cat to love. Travel through bad weather. Avoid little yappy dogs, and wild calico cats. Be patient. Keep looking.

$\mathcal{L}eo$

Of all the cats I have known, Leo, most of all, seemed to have an agenda, a plan for what he wanted to do. Easy-going and extremely popular with other cats, Leo first appeared at our door in the city convent when he was an adolescent. Based on his coloring and patterned markings, Leo was obviously related to the majority of neighborhood cats.

Every night Leo stopped at the back door, waiting for his cat food dinner. If we were late, Leo just patiently waited—other cats usually moved on to search for dinner elsewhere, but not Leo. Almost as if he knew we would not be gone overnight, he waited, watching the back door.

Of course, we tried to trap Leo—to bring him inside if possible, but if not, at least to have him neutered and vaccinated. Sometimes Leo spent the days sleeping, hidden under the hollyhocks in the side yard. On other days, he explored more distant areas of the neighborhood. Perhaps Leo had watched other cats be caught in the Haravart trap, but for whatever reason, Leo only looked at the trap and walked around it.

Leo was not actually very wild—we could almost just walk over to him and pick him up. But not quite! Leo watched carefully, and at the last moment, he darted away.

Once I put a dish of cat food on the back steps and another just inside the door. I propped the door open, thinking that maybe Leo would just come in on his own. But no. He ate the food on the steps, and then walked calmly away.

I knew that Leo did not like the rain and did not like getting wet. Once during a heavy downpour, Leo had crept very close to the back door, but then just when I thought he would slip inside the screen door, the rain suddenly stopped! Leo found a shelter from the dripping dampness under a large hollyhock leaf.

As summer turned to fall, Leo's coat grew thicker. He stayed close to the house and even sat on the door mat when the weather was cool. He followed the sunshine—Leo, I surmised, wanted to stay warm. I hoped that he would have a warm place to spend the winter.

I need not have worried about Leo at all. An early November evening brought a wet, blustery snow. I opened the back door to put dinner out for the neighborhood cats, and there was Leo. Without a moment's hesitation, he darted in through the door!

Leo, who of course had never been in our house, ran through the entrance area and kitchen, past the dinning room, right into the living room. He lay down, curled on a small rug, as though he knew exactly where he was and what he was doing.

I followed him into the living room. "Welcome to Sanctuary House, Little One," I said. Leo just looked up at me, a serious cat expression on his face.

I leaned over and scooped him into my arms. Leo is

a small, compact cat. He snuggled, leaning right into my chest, burying his face in my blue apron.

"I'm glad to be here," he seemed to say. "I just wanted to wait until it got cold to come in!"

Leo now lives in the cat courtyard. He is friendly and peaceful. All of the other cats love him—and, no little surprise, so do the Sisters.

Lucie

 ucie came to Sanctuary House when we still lived in the city. One night, just at dusk, she came walking up the driveway to the area where we left food for the regular neighborhood cats. We had never seen Lucie before. She was extremely thin and bedraggled—she looked as though she had been on the losing side of a fight. And she was dirty! Her normally white fur was gray with dirt and oil. We suspected that she had been living under a nearby abandoned building or around the corner at an engine repair shop. But wherever she had been, Lucie had not been cared for. She was covered with fleas, and was actually starving. Even the other cats stepped back from her, not because she hissed or growled at them, but simply because she was a stranger, and a rather unpleasant stranger at that.

Usually, when cats have been out for any length of time, as apparently this one had, they are skitterish and wary of people, but not Lucie. She came right up to Sister Harriet and me and rubbed against our legs. When I sat on the steps near the back door, she tried to get in my lap.

There was only one thing to do. We took Lucie in and made a safe place for her apart from the other cats and, of course, applied anti-flea drops! The next morning I took her to see the vet. He confirmed our belief that Lucie was starving, but also gave us the good news that she had no other physical problems.

I called the cat Lucie because, while she was quite young, something about her—her white fur and blue eyes, I think—reminded me of my elderly Aunt Lucie, who had white hair and blue eyes. Lucie responded to her name almost immediately.

For a very long time it seemed that Lucie was starved not only for food, but also for affection. She liked nothing better than sitting in my lap, or on top of the computer where she could offer a helping paw, or between person and book or newspaper. Gradually, Lucie also became friends with the other cats at Sanctuary House, and needed less one-on-one human attention. She and Gracie alternate between being best of friends and totally annoying playmates. She plays chase with Caroline and stretches out for a nap with Tip or Leo. And with me—well, Lucie is content with a very few minutes of attention, preferring a head rub to being held. She usually comes to greet me, but is satisfied with a brief, "Hello, Lucie!"

Today Lucie lives in the cat courtyard. She has put on weight, and her white fur with red gold markings is healthy and thick. Lucie has bright blue Siamese eyes, but is not talkative. Unlike many white, blue-eyed cats, she can hear perfectly well—and like all cats, she can ignore my calling her name perfectly well too!

Maggie

Sister Harriet called from church, "Do you think we have room for another cat or two? One of the parishioners has two cats that her neighbor left when she moved to Canada."

We felt sad and, of course, sympathetic for the poor abandoned cats. Both were adults, and no doubt had trusted their person to care for them always. Sister brought the cats home: Chip, a friendly orange and white cat; and Furbie, a shy distant calico of muted colors.

Although they had belonged to the same woman, the two cats did not know each other. Chip had been a strictly outdoor cat, and Furbie had lived inside. I made a telephone call to a woman who had recently lost her cat.

She was delighted to hear about Chip. He immediately began playing with her two young twins, and they took him home. Chip had reminded me of Thomas so much that I hated to see him leave, but I knew he was going to a wonderful, caring home, and I was happy for him.

Furbie, on the other hand, was not such a friendly cat. She positively was not going home with any children—in fact, she wasn't even going to let them touch her! No question about it, she was not a good adoption candidate.

For a cat who had lived a rather pampered life indoors, Furbie made a quick adjustment to the cat courtyard.

Sister Harriet and I looked at Furbie and then at each other. "I don't think her name is really Furbie," Sister Harriet said. "She's a MagnifiCat. Let's call her Maggie."

Surprising though it sounds, Maggie responded the first time we said her name. "You really are Maggie," I said.

Maggie's favorite spot in the cat courtyard is on the

brick steps, near the back door. Sitting on the top step puts her just a little higher than everyone else, and this is exactly where she feels she belongs! Maggie would like to be in charge of every cat, deciding who eats when and supervising play and rest times.

For a long time, Patrick, the true alpha cat, just let her pretend to be in charge. Gray Gracie, and more recently calico Abbie, are her greatest rivals for alpha female—the three of them have made a tentative truce!

Magnificent, MagnifiCat—Maggie!

Mari

*M*ari couldn't really remember what happened. He did remember that he was a little tiny kitten, with kitten brothers and sisters, and that they ran and played together, and drank warm milk from their mother. And he did remember running through the grass after a butterfly, and chasing his tail around and around, and hiding under the porch while the other kittens looked for him. And, most of all, Mari did remember that he had been given a great gift—God's special gift to cats—he could purr.

He purred when he was happy, when he snuggled against his mother, when he tumbled and played with his sisters and brothers, and most of all when he felt safe and content.

But one day, someone grabbed him roughly, and cut off his tail, and dropped him beside the steps. Mari was very afraid. His mother and brothers and sisters had run away. Mari was all alone. The little stub that used to be his tail was bleeding. Mari was afraid and very, very hurt and lonely. He could only make a little "mew" sound, and didn't know if he wanted anyone to come or not.

And, in those few minutes, Mari lost his purr. Mari sat very still and waited; he was very quiet. He tried to hide behind a flower pot, but it hurt when he moved. It was starting to get dark and cold, and he couldn't even think any little kitten thoughts any more—and he certainly couldn't purr.

And that is where I found Mari.

I scooped him up and wrapped him in a towel. Mari was afraid, but he was too tired and too hurt to move or even make a sound. I washed his stub of a tail and then carefully lifted him into a box. He was still too afraid and too hurt to move or make a sound.

I took Mari to the vet, who confirmed that his missing tail had been chopped off. No stitches were needed, but the vet prescribed antibiotics and quiet rest. The next day, I took Mari home and made a special place of his own away from the other cats. Mari settled in and eventually slept for a long time, but he never made a sound.

When Mari woke up again the sun was coming in through the windows. He was still curled tightly in his box, but he felt warm and hungry, and his tail did not hurt so much.

He could hear me talking to the other cats and tried to get in the very corner of the box so that I couldn't see him. He was very quiet so I wouldn't hear him. He didn't want to be touched. He wanted to hide, so no one could ever hurt him again. Mari tried to hide under the blanket in his box, but really there was no place to hide.

I took Mari a saucer of food and a clean blanket, and spoke to him in a very soft, sing-song voice.

Mari was hungry, but he didn't want to be touched, so he hissed and reached out his paw and extended his tiny claws. I didn't try to pet Mari.

Mari knew I was in the room, but he never looked at me—he just watched from the sides of his eyes without moving at all, and without making a sound. All day I stayed near, but did not touch the kitten.

In Mari's mind, even though his little tail stub did not hurt any more, he did not ever want anyone to touch him again. People were too big and too rough; Mari was very small but he could hiss and scratch—that is how he would keep everyone away. And he would never purr.

Every day I took Mari food and a clean blanket, and always talked to him: "You're a good kitten, Mari. You're safe now. No one will hurt you."

Mari listened, but he didn't make a sound; he certainly didn't purr.

Sometimes I played soft music, and I gave Mari two toys, a white cardboard butterfly with green ribbon wings, and a fluffy blue pillow. Mari leaned against the pillow, and when he thought I wasn't looking he chased the butterfly, scooting it across the floor. But Mari didn't purr.

And then, little by little, Mari decided that he was not so afraid.

First, he didn't try to hide when I came into the room. Then he looked at me. Then he let me touch him. But still he didn't purr.

Then one day, Mari let me see him play with the butterfly.

And finally, he let me pick him up! "I love you, Mari," I said.

At first Mari was very still, he almost didn't breathe, but he could feel my heart beat when I held him close to my chest.

I rubbed his head and his ears—Mari remembered his mother and brothers and sisters.

Mari felt safe and happy and content again.

Then slowly, very slowly, he began to purr.

Today, Mari lives in the cat courtyard at Sanctuary House. Thanks to Nori he learned to trust and love other cats. His special friends are Theo, Ari, and Moses. He is still painfully shy and elusive around humans—but when he is very happy and feels safe, he does purr.

Mira and Goldie

Mira and Goldie are the daughters of Sofie and—we think—Solomon. For kittens born just a few minutes apart, they are very different in many respects. Mira, whose real name is Myrrh, is a brilliant calico, exactly like her mother. Goldie, whose real name is Gold, is the color of winter straw, exactly like her father. Like most calico cats, Mira is very independent and self-assured, just like her mother; Goldie is more cautious, just like her father. Mira loves to be in the courtyard, chasing dragonflies and butterflies and leaves in the day, and staring at the stars at night. Goldie, on the other hand, prefers to stay inside, watching the wind blow the tree leaves from her perch on the window sill.

In many important respects Mira and Goldie are very similar. Both are gentle and loving cats. They get along well with other cats and with dogs, and are happy to cuddle. Mira enjoys being a lap cat, and Goldie's favorite place to sleep at night is on top of my head or curled against my neck. Both Mira and Goldie have lean, sleek bodies, and both run, jump, and leap with abandon. And most important of all, Mira and Goldie have a mysterious ability to communicate.

Of course, all cats—well, all animals—can communicate with humans if we only pay careful attention. But Mira and Goldie have honed their communication skills to perfection. They know how to make eye contact and stare intently; they are masters of the silent meow—and the vocal meow, too! They know when to purr, and when to bury their faces in the crook of an arm or neck. And what do they think? What message is in their cat minds?—"It's marvelously fun to be a cat!"

Moses and Aaron

No two cats could be closer than Moses and Aaron—or Ari—two brother cats who first visited our in-town Sanctuary House as young adolescents. I have no idea where the two leggy kittens came from, but one morning when I went outside, there they were. Their markings are quite similar in pattern although they are different colors: Moses is white with bright orange and butterscotch swirls; Ari is white with black and tan swirls.

The kittens were leery of people, but they were hungry. I fed them and managed to catch them. Both were neutered and given shots. We wanted to keep them indoors, but they soon made it clear that they preferred the outside. They raced around, jumping and swinging from curtains, knocking over a book case, and lunging at the window screens. With only a moment's hesitation, I opened the door and let them back outside!

Ari is slightly larger than Moses and is a more sedate cat. Moses is an aerial acrobat! He often appeared at my second floor window, placidly watching me. But when I opened the window to let him in, he was gone in a flash. He could only have gotten to the second floor by climbing the tree next door, jumping over to the garage roof, and from there climbing onto the second floor overhang. It was an amazing feat, and one he rehearsed almost every day.

When we were preparing to move from the town to our present Sanctuary House, I managed to once again trap both cats. By now they were full grown, but just as feral as ever as far as people were concerned. I put them on the L-shaped screen porch, but could not catch them a third time, even within this relatively confined space. It began to occur to me that perhaps they would be better left in the city neighborhood where they had grown up. I knew that ours was not the only house where they had food left out for them—perhaps another person would have better luck caring for them.

When we had removed all of the other cats waiting to go to our new home, I opened one of the windows on the porch and Moses scooted out. Ari, who was sitting on top of a stack of furniture, just stared down at me. He appeared to be completely nonchalant, as if I had interrupted his morning nap.

"Okay, Ari," I said, "I'm going to work. I'll be back at noon; you just do whatever you want to do, but tomorrow we're moving, and you will have to live somewhere else."

Ari closed his eyes and put his head between his front paws. He knew that I couldn't possibly reach him—he was completely in charge and loving it!

When I returned home for lunch, I was sure that Ari

would have followed Moses outside. I went to the porch to lower the window. Ari was sitting on the window sill. He hopped down—inside! I held an open cat carrier in front of him and he walked right in, satisfied, I suppose, that I had remembered not to touch him!

That afternoon, we took Ari and several boxes of books and two chairs to the new house, where he quickly and happily joined his former cat acquaintances in the courtyard. Sister Harriet stayed at the new house, and I returned to the old house to be there for the furniture movers who would come the next morning.

The old house felt hollow. Almost all of the furniture had been moved downstairs, and everything easily transported by car had been already taken away. I walked through the house, my steps making an echoing sound, checking cabinets and closets one last time, and then settled down for an early night of sleep, the last night in my second floor bedroom.

About midnight, I was awakened by a loud and persistent, "Meow!" It sounded like Moses, but surely he had not come back. I turned on the light and opened the window. There he was—my silly orange and white cat! He calmly stepped right inside.

The next morning, he too, like his brother Ari, walked into the cat carrier that I held open for him.

Now, Moses and Ari are very much at home in the cat courtyard at Sanctuary House. Moses sometimes sleeps in the cat house, but Ari always sleeps outside—under the stars in good weather, or under the cat house when it rains. Usually they are close together, sometimes doing the exact same thing, at other times mirroring each other, with one going to the right and the other to the left. They are extremely popular with the other cats, but never allow me to touch them or even get close enough to reach them.

I have learned to accept Moses and Aaron as they are. They have not asked me to change my personality, and I will not ask them to change theirs. We may not always understand each other, but respect, love, and admiration—yes, we do have those!

Murphy, Josie, and Sully

The Triplets

A friend called me about a garage sale on her street. "I think they have bird cages and cat carriers," she said. That sounded too good to miss, so within an hour I found myself searching through the odds and ends of a neighborhood sale.

There was a bird cage, but I decided it was too small, and a cat carrier, which I purchased—fortunately, because lurking in a corner, I found three kittens! Old enough to be away from their mother, but not really old enough to be entirely on their own, they sat huddled together, watching the negotiations.

"Are those your kittens?" I asked the man with the cash box.

"Nope," he replied curtly. "You can have them if you want them, otherwise I'm taking them to the humane society. I would have taken their mother, too, but I couldn't find her."

Needless to say, I wanted the kittens. The first two were easy to catch—the third one decided we were playing a game and raced around the garage, over and under boxes of trinkets, lawn and garden implements, and anything else scattered about.

At last, after a half hour of "playing," I had all three kittens safely in the carrier. Even for someone with many cats, I would have to say that these three kittens were the most beautiful ones I had ever seen. All three had long hair and had a delicate but aristocratic aura.

The first was white and orange, his orange ears uniquely outlined in white; the second was a muted salmon color—a "pink" kitty, as my friend Susan said; the third was brilliant, dark orange, with a white vest and paws.

My neighbors, Sue and Bob, fell in love with the kittens as quickly as I had. We thought they were all three girls and gave them names from Gilbert and Sullivan operettas—Mabel, Josephine or "Josie," and Phoebe. Bob and Sue wanted to adopt Mabel, and I was certain that the other two, such beautiful kittens, would soon have adoptive homes as well. The kittens were not only beautiful, but also energetic and affectionate.

I took the kittens to the vet for their first shots and we encountered two surprises. First, Mabel and Phoebe were boys—they were quickly renamed Murphy and Sully. The second surprise was a sad one: all three tested positive for feline AIDS.

My resolve never to take in sick cats or kittens melted. I couldn't ask the vet to euthanize them—nor was he willing to do that. We agreed to re-test them in six months, hoping that they merely had antibodies from their mother, and that they themselves would be healthy once their own immune systems developed.

In the meantime, I moved the kittens into the guest bedroom, away from any other cats. Bob and Sue, who also have other cats, still came to play with the kittens, but knew that they might never be able to take Murphy home with them.

The kittens grew and flourished over the next months. They chased each other and played rough and tumble games over and under the bed. They had all shapes and sizes of cat toys which they regularly hid under the dresser.

We estimated that they were six months old in December, but I waited until almost February before taking them to be re-tested. By this time, of course, I had decided to keep them, no matter what—they could have the guest room permanently, if necessary!

I held my breath and said a silent prayer as the vet drew blood from each kitten and put it in the test kit. And, miracle of miracles, all three kittens proved healthy!

Murphy, Josie, and Sully have grown into gentle, affectionate cats. Murphy has gone home with his much-loved Sue and Bob. Josie and Sully are very popular with the other Sanctuary House cats, and will be

staying right here. Sully loves to be in the cat courtyard where he can lie on his back and watch clouds
and birds over head. Josie's favorite game is hide-and-
seek; her choice of hiding place is always the second
shelf in the linen closet! You can find her there most
mornings, just waiting to be found.

[This story was first published in *Cats & Kittens* magazine in January 2005.]

Noah

Two days after little Rosie and Zoë came to Sanctuary House, a third kitten, rescued after Hurricane Isabel, joined our family. Noah—we named him since he had survived the flood—is gray and white. He was older than the other two kittens, really an adolescent. The people on Taylors Island found him going from door to door, looking for his home, but no one claimed him. Possibly the house where he lived before the hurricane had been completely flooded; many people had to move at least temporarily from the island—perhaps his people were gone. The young cat seemed dazed and was very withdrawn and quiet when he arrived.

In time, however, Noah became more outgoing. He

developed a great friendship with Inky and the two play cat soccer every day! I had assumed that Noah would want to be in the cat courtyard, where he would have more space and team members for cat games, and for a few hours, I was right. Noah ran in and out of the cat house, and walked along the paving stone borders of the flower beds. He hid in a large clump of mint and jumped out on Leo and Caroline. But then, he wanted to come back indoors to play with Inky— and I was not there to let him in!

The north side of the cat courtyard is fenced by the main house, and three large windows open from the house onto the courtyard. Once, Lucie had jumped onto the screen in one window, almost by mistake. But now Noah saw the screens as the best way into the house. He didn't know, of course, that there was glass behind the screens, or maybe encountering glass in the first window, he had hoped there was no glass in the others. In any event, I came home to find the screens shredded!

"What would you have done in a big flood?" I asked

him. "What if you had been with the original Noah on the ark, captive for all those days?"

"But I wasn't on an ark," he thought back at me. "I just want to go find Inky. It's time for cat soccer!"

Nori

$\mathcal{L}$ong-haired, gray and white, green-eyed, beautiful Nori appeared most unexpectedly one night. I had put out a Havahart trap, hoping to catch a cat who had been coming for food for several weeks—but instead of that cat, I caught Nori. I had never seen her in our neighborhood before, and thinking she might belong to someone else, I opened the trap to let her go, and even turned it on one end, but she clung to the wires of the cage, unwilling to leave the can of cat food that I had used as bait. Even when the food was gone, she would not get out of the trap until I took her into the house.

In the kitchen, Nori stepped shyly into the light, staring warily at the cabinets, stove, refrigerator, dishwasher, table and chairs. She ate almost another full can of food and immediately fell asleep in a towel-lined box I had put in the corner. She was thin and somewhat unkempt, a young adult, not spayed—amazingly, she was not pregnant!

Of course, her name was not Nori when I first met her. I called her Gray Kitty, and then decided that she, too, like all of our cats at that point, needed a "Canterbury Tail" name. With no female Archbishops of Canterbury, it was again necessary to invent a feminine name from a masculine one, as I had done by using Michael Ramsey's name for Michaela "Tip" and St. Augustine's name for Augusta "Gussie." At the time this little gray cat came to our house, George Leonard Carey was the Archbishop of Canterbury, so I name her Lenore, and then quickly shortened her name to Nori.

Nori was the first long-haired cat to come to Sanctuary House, and although she was as strong and feisty as every other feline member of our household, she looked more delicate and dainty. Sometimes, with the other cats, she could be rather demanding. She wanted to be held and petted, and did not wish to share any human's attention with other cats! And so it was a great surprise that Nori was also one of the most generous and least self-centered cats that I have ever known.

Summer changed to fall. Nori had lived with us for a few months and had established her place with the other cats, when I came home one day to find a tiny injured kitten on the back steps. The kitten had been cruelly and intentionally hurt. He was in shock and was too frightened to move. I rushed him to the vet, who was able to save him.

When the kitten, Mari, came home, he had to have a week of quiet and complete rest, apart from the other cats. I tried to talk quietly to him, but he would not look at me and was rigid when I tried to pick him up. I knew that the kitten would heal physically, but wondered if he would ever relate to anyone else—person or cat.

Eventually I discovered that I need not have worried

about Mari with the other cats. All of the cats accepted him, most of them just giving him an introductory sniff. Nori, however, rubbed against the tiny kitten, and then lay down on her side. He buried his face in her long fur and began to suck on a nipple. Of course, Nori had no milk for the kitten, but that didn't seem to bother either of them.

Nori allowed Mari to nurse for weeks until gradually he no longer needed to be lost in her fur. After almost two months, she finally pushed him away. They remain friends, but strictly as adult cats. Actually, although Mari is still wary of humans, he has an excellent friendship with all of our cats.

Nori, too, is well-loved by the other cats. And if she sometimes she needs special attention and her own space, that is fine with me!

Patrick
(1996-2004)

The big tabby kitten loped awkwardly across the street, slightly dragging his rear left leg. He stopped in front of our house and sat down. It was a very hot day and the kitten was out of breath. I scooped him up. "You're not safe here," I said. "There are too many cars for a kitten to avoid. Come have a drink of water and let me see what is wrong with your leg."

The kitten curled into my arms. He was not heavy, but big boned, and he was very hot, hungry and thirsty! I could feel no broken bones or other injury to his leg, and he didn't seem to be in any pain. He panted, then finally fell asleep, exhausted, in the breeze of our overhead fan.

The next morning I took the kitten to the vet, who carefully examined his leg. "It's not an injury," he told me, "only poor nutrition. With a good diet he'll be fine."

I left the kitten at the vet's for a few days so that his diet and weight could be closely monitored. I thought that the kitten would be quickly adopted, and even called a friend who had recently lost her cat. I described the kitten—his beautiful tabby stripes and his affectionate personality. My friend agreed to go with me to see the kitten.

Together we went into the kennel section of the vet's office where I lifted the kitten from his cage. He climbed into my arms and reached his front paws up to my cheeks, then he stretched up and rubbed his face on mine.

"He's your kitten," my friend laughed. "I couldn't possibly take him!"

And I was very glad she said that, because I couldn't possibly have parted with him either!

I brought the kitten home and we named him

Patrick after St. Patrick of Ireland. The vet was right—Patrick's lame leg grew strong with proper diet. However, whether as a result of his poor nourishment as a kitten or for some other, unknown, reason, Patrick continued to have many physical problems. He never lost his sweet, patient temperament though.

For a long time, Patrick lived in the cat courtyard, where among his many cat friends, he was the undisputed alpha cat. Patrick was a huge cat, weighing over 20 pounds. He was much larger than most of the other cats, but was a gentle giant in dealing with them, a benevolent dictator. He had an on-going love affair with food, and as the alpha cat, always ate first. If any other cat questioned this arrangement, Patrick calmly reached out his paw and rested it on the questioner's head. I never saw him hurt another cat—he just reminded them of the correct cat order.

As the years went on, Patrick developed diabetes. He spent two weeks boarding at our vet's office, with every bit of food carefully regulated. The hope was that by guarding his diet, we could control his diabetes without medication. Patrick loved the clinic—he was in cool air conditioned splendor, and had a ring-side seat for supervising the comings and goings of the other patients. He was a favorite with the staff and often reached out a paw, beckoning Judy or Audrey to his cage for an affectionate rub behind his ears.

When his blood sugar stabilized, he was allowed to come home. He was happy, and healthier than he had been for some time. He stayed indoors, where he and Izzy quickly agreed to share the downstairs areas. Patrick, who had never watched television, soon discovered that he could join me on the couch for BBC America entertainment—perhaps he did not understand the dialog, but he knew that he liked being in my lap or close beside me.

A few days later, on a hot, humid summer morning he came into the kitchen and flopped down on the floor, panting heavily. I called the vet, certain that this was not a symptom of diabetes, but not sure what was wrong. These were symptoms that were completely new for Patrick. The vet suggested moving him into an air conditioned room. I put him in an upstairs bedroom, with cool air and plenty of cold water to drink. At first I put him on the bed, but he opted to lie on the floor. I offered him food and water, which he refused. I brought one of his best cat friends from the courtyard. Leo sat next to Patrick for a minute, ate the food, and then let me know that he wanted to go back outside.

In an hour Patrick was no better. His breathing was still labored. When he stood up, he made a loud groaning noise, as if the effort were too much for him. Our emergency vet was away for the day, so I lifted Patrick into the car for the long drive to Easton.

X-rays and an EKG revealed a collapsed lung and cardiomyopathy, a serious heart condition. The doctor began quickly naming treatments and medications that might help.

"Wait," I said, "is this for my benefit?"

"Yes," came the reply. "Patrick will never be well. He might live for six months or six hours; you can take him home, but he could die at any time. And this is a painful death."

I remembered Rudy's seizures and screams when he had died of the same heart disease. I looked at Patrick's face, already twisted in pain, and listened to his labored breathing, I cradled his face in my hands as he had once held my cheeks between his paws.

"I love you Patrick," I whispered. "You don't have to hurt any more now. You go to sleep. Go find Rudy and Alistair; we'll come later. Tippy, Theo, Sasha, and I... all of us. We'll catch up with you later."

Patrick will always have a special place in my heart—after all he reached out his paws and rested them on my head too!

Quin

*I*t was a cold, wet night, with rain turning to sleet. I had just closed the cover to the hens' coop, when I saw a slight movement in the weeds at the edge of the fence. I thought it might be a mouse, and reached over to encourage it to stay away from the hens. Much to my surprise, I heard a faint mew sound—there was a tiny, tabby kitten. I saw the mother cat in the distance, and hoped that she would not move other kittens with this one. It did look like a safe place, sheltered on one side by a brick wall, and under a tarp... but that was only if the hens were not there. A hen could and would easily kill and eat a kitten this small.

I took the kitten inside. She was covered with fleas

and was icy cold. Gradually, the kitten began to warm—I wanted to feed her, but knew that she could not eat until she was closer to normal temperature. I went out to check on other possible kittens, but there were none.

The kitten was only a day or two old; her eyes were shut tight and her ears were folded close to her head. Finally, she was able to drink the formula I had mixed. I fed her every two hours and was thrilled that she survived the night.

For the next few weeks, I took the kitten everywhere with me; when my newspaper job interfered with kitten care, I left her with "Aunt Susan" and "Aunt Judy" at the veterinary office. The kitten was so tiny that our guesses of male or female were just that—guesses! One day we said, "Oh, it's a girl," and the next "I think it's a boy."

"Ask Eddie," Susan said, "he's the vet!"

"Female," he answered confidently. "Probably," he added cautiously.

"Well this kitten needs a name," I persisted.

"So think of a person you admire," Judy suggested, "and give the kitten that person's last name. That way you'll have a unisex name—you can't go wrong."

That was easy. I immediately thought of Clinton Quin, a former Episcopal Bishop of Texas. "Then the kitten is named Quin," I said.

"The mighty Quin," Judy said.

We were concerned that Quin, growing up without a mother cat or sibling kittens, might become anti-social, so we tried to let her have play time with other cats. Gracie and Caroline wanted nothing to do with her, but Leo proved to be an excellent babysitter.

Quin has grown up to be a very small cat. She is the most acrobatic cat at Sanctuary House. Even as a very young kitten she could balance on the round dowels of the quilt stand, and as soon as she discovered how to jump, she taught herself to scale the door frame. But Quin's most outstanding eccentricity is the way she talks to herself; she growls and screeches as though she were in a huge cat fight! When she first began doing this, I often rushed upstairs expecting to see fur flying—but no other cats were involved at all. Quin was just chasing her own tail or pretending to fight! She sounds quite fierce—all of the Sanctuary House dogs have barked at her, even howled, in response to her screeches. Now, after two years, they, like the cats, ignore her! But I don't think she cares. Quin is an actress, a prima donna—a mighty Quin, indeed.

Ragu

*Y*es, the correct, by-the-book spelling would be "Ragout," but to simplify everything we borrowed a spaghetti sauce spelling. Really though, it doesn't matter, because at Sanctuary House, our Ragu is just called Goo.

Goo was born on a farm, under the back porch steps, but was soon adopted and moved to a more city-like atmosphere where she grew into a beautiful, strong, long-haired calico. Life was stable and happy, until her elderly owner was taken to the hospital. Goo was taken to be boarded at the vet's office.

At first, Goo didn't mind this arrangement. She is a quiet, reserved cat, and life in a cage was not all that bad. She had excellent food, a soft blanket, and plenty of attention from the staff. And there was entertainment, too—all day long, different cats and dogs came and went—Goo watched in fascination, safe in her own private cubbyhole.

Of course, Goo was hoping and planning to return home, but that was not to happen. In fact, Goo would not see her person again in this life, for the woman died in the hospital. Goo became a ward of the Animal Clinic of Talbot.

In this new phase of Goo's life, she actually acquired a job. She became a blood donor, a life saver for cats who had been injured or who, for whatever reason, needed a blood transfusion. Goo was happy to do this—after all, the procedure was painless to her, and she was always rewarded with extra food and special treats! Being a wise cat who had witnessed many hurt or sick cats come and go, Goo realized, at some level, that she was crucial to the whole operation. The vet needed her as much as she needed him; they were partners in saving lives and in treating, maybe even in curing, disease! Any cat can donate blood one time to any other cat, and Goo sometimes wondered how many cats now shared a little of her spirit.

Eventually, as Goo got older, she was less enthusiastic about going to work—even the constant entertainment outside her cubbyhole home was becoming boring. Susan and I often talked about the best options for Goo. We held her close to our hearts and listened to what she was telling us, both of us trying to understand what Goo really wanted. And so, after many long discussions with and about Goo, she moved to Sanctuary House.

At first, this was not an easy transition. Suddenly she had to share a room with all manner of cats—an old one, kittens, and even the screecher Quin! However, drawing on her inner strength and hearty calico legacy, Goo has made an excellent adjustment.

For a long time Goo sat on the window sill, staring out at the trees shading the cat courtyard, but an actual visit to the courtyard convinced her that it should remain a virtual experience; she has been an indoor cat for many years, and only wanted to see the world outside, not live in it again. For an older cat, who had not had much playtime, chasing felt mice and paper butterflies is just as exciting as finding real bugs and butterflies in the courtyard. For a cat who had been in a cage, birds through the window are as exciting as birds without the window there.

Very early one morning I woke up to find Goo snuggled in the crook of my arm. She was kneading her paws against my side and sucking on the sleeve of my nightshirt. "Goo?" I said.

She looked up at me. "I am a beautiful grown-up cat," she thought. "I have saved lives and done quietly heroic deeds. Now, I am home safe. I want to snuggle and be loved and I will love you forever in return."

"Yes, Goo," I whispered. "I love you and you are home!"

Rosie & Zoë

𝒻riends, cleaning up after the floods of Hurricane Isabel, called me from Taylors Island. They had found two tiny kittens on top of a barrel surrounded by tidal flood water. The mother cat, perhaps drowned, had not come for them—nor could she reach them if she did return.

Of course, I agreed to take the kittens. They were very thin and malnourished; their fur was rough and even missing on the ends of their tails—but both were calico! One, with distinct, bright colors, I named Zoë, a name beginning with Z to remember our old horse, Zuma, who had died just the day before. From the very first, Zoë looked up at me when I whispered her name. She knows exactly who she is! The other kitten, darker and more pastel, turned her tiny face toward me and stared into my eyes. "My name is Rosie," she thought. "Rosie," I whispered to her.

Both kittens grew strong and healthy. Healthy, that is, until Rosie became very ill with fever, vomiting and diarrhea. In just two days her weight dropped from three pounds to two. Our vet sent a prescription for her—she was easy to medicate, but was eating almost nothing. Rosie's condition went from bad to worse as she had a completely negative reaction to the medicine. She was limp, comatose, and I was afraid she was going to die.

I drove her to the vet's office, all the way trying to convince myself that if she could not get well then it would be right to euthanize her. I didn't want her to suffer, and she seemed incredibly frail and weak. The vet felt her pulse and listened to her heart. "She's going to be alright," he said. "Her heart is strong." Her reaction to the medication was not a common one, but was certainly a recognized caution in a small percentage of cats. She was deeply asleep. I took her home with subcutaneous fluids and an alternate medication.

For the next 24 hours I could hardly believe that Rosie would survive—she remained limp and unresponsive. But I kept remembering that she had a strong heartbeat. I slept in a chair, keeping her close beside me.

And then, miraculously, she woke up! She took a few stumbling steps, and then quickly regained her balance. She nuzzled my hand and licked a little cat food from a saucer.

Rosie was definitely back; happily, Zoë didn't devleop the same illness.

Rosie and Zoë are almost grown-up cats now. Zoë, the more adventurous of the two, instantly loved being in the cat courtyard, where she can run and play with many other cats. She jumps at bugs and butterflies, chases and is chased by Lucie and Caroline, and plays rough and tumble cat games with Leo, Tut, Henry, and Mira.

Rosie visited the courtyard and eventually decided that she, too, would rather live there than indoors. She is—like Zoë—a high-energy cat, always running, jumping, racing, pouncing, and leaping. She would like to be in charge, but Abbie, Sofie, and Maggie have convinced her that she had better put that idea in the back of her cat mind, at least for the present time!

Ruby

The first time I saw Ruby she was a tiny kitten, sitting in the doorway of an abandoned building. The weather was rainy and very cold. Ruby's long, dark fur was coated with a thin layer of ice—she sparkled like a snow flake! I tried to catch her, but she darted into the bushes near the doorway.

Soon, I began seeing Ruby and her identical brother Rudy in our yard. Ruby, like Rudy, was extremely shy, but eventually I did catch her. While Ruby was at the vet's office to be spayed, a client who had recently lost her cat, saw her and immediately wanted to adopt her.

Most of the cats who come to live at Sanctuary House are not adoptable, but Ruby was healthy and young, and it seemed that she would have excellent care with the woman who wanted take her home. As an only cat, she would have a lot of attention and love—she would have a special place in a good home.

Ruby's adoptive family seemed to be just right for her. She loved the wife and two young boys, who adored her in return. But then there was the husband of the family.

Whether Ruby did not like him in particular, or did not like men in general, she never did say, but in the way that cats have of letting everyone know their displeasure, Ruby stopped using the litter box.

We have an agreement with all adoptive families that any unwanted adoptee must be returned to us. Within a few weeks, Ruby was back at Sanctuary House.

The cats, especially her brother Rudy, and I were delighted to have her back home. Ruby and Rudy ran and wrestled together, often tumbling into a heap of dark brown and black fur. The only way to tell them apart was that Rudy had a slightly crooked ear—the result of a fight before he came to Sanctuary House.

Ruby has never neglected the litter box again, so I believe she must be exactly where she wants to be.

Ruby especially enjoys being in the cat courtyard. Although she is rather small for a mostly Maine Coon cat, she is a strong, independent girl who loves to chase butterflies and leaves and other cats! She really seems to like cold weather and is one of the last cats to move into the heated cat house in the winter.

Last year, Ruby's brother died unexpectedly—the cats seemed to know no more about his mysterious illness than I did. At first, Ruby seemed very lonely, but now she is quite at home with her other cat siblings.

And we—well, we all are very glad to have Ruby home again!

Rudy
(1998-2003)

Rudy was obviously descended from a Maine Coon cat or two. A strong, elegant cat with huge green-gold eyes and a long tabby coat, he roamed our backyard, coming and going over the high wooden fence. He was shy, evasive, silent, and although he always seemed to know who was in the yard, he never made eye contact. If he was in the yard when we went out, he did not run, but merely crouched under the forsythia bush, waiting for us to leave so that he could reclaim his realm.

I had once caught him. He was neutered and provided with all recommended shots, but he was wild, and I let him go back into the yard. I fed him every day, remarked on his beauty, respected his wild independence. And, of course, I worried about him; I was glad when he finally decided that he did not need to leave our yard. Only when we were preparing to move did I catch him again, update his immunizations and enclose him on our long, L-shaped porch.

When moving day came, he defiantly refused to be caught. For almost two hours I chased him as he deftly jumped from packing box to furniture, and easily wiggled away when I almost caught him. I gave up and opened the window. "Okay," I sighed. "Go on, you can go out. You can stay here."

Rudy looked at me, eyes wide and staring, from the top of a dresser. He didn't move. I walked over and picked him up. "You're crazy," I told him.

Rudy easily adapted to our new home, where along with the courtyard the cats enjoy a sheltered area and several "dog" houses and a golf-umbrella shaded spot. The other cats loved Rudy. His identical sister, Ruby, had lived at Sanctuary House for a long time, and she quickly re-established their close ties. Some of our cats had known Rudy from the "street;" others met him as though he were a long-lost friend. Rudy did not trust or love people, but he adored and was adored by other cats. He rubbed against them, shared their food dishes, and curled up with them to sleep in the sun.

Some things about Rudy did not change with the move. He still avoided being touched or picked up, preferring just to watch me from across the courtyard. If I interrupted any cat games, he quickly dashed behind the rose bush or into the mint, watching until I left his space. He watched the other cats being held or brushed, but never came close enough to share in those activities. He didn't completely hide, but he was aloof, standoffish, and silent.

On Rudy's annual visit to the vet, a mouth infection required that he spend several nights away from home. I knew that he was angry and in pain. Once back home, however, he greeted Ruby and the other cats with gusto. We had our most hands-on experience of a life time, as I gave him his antibiotic drops morning and evening, and I think both of us were glad when, mouth healed, he could again avoid being held.

We easily slipped into our old routine. From the window, I could watch Rudy play tag with the other cats or chase leaves or wrestle with Ruby, but when I went out to the courtyard, he stopped playing and retreated. A few times I tried to go near him. "Come on, Rudy, please play," I coaxed.

"No way," he stared back distantly. But at least he's making eye contact, I thought, maybe, just maybe someday Rudy will want to be petted and loved, too.

But then one night, when I had gone to the courtyard to tell the cats goodnight, I heard a crying moan. I quickly counted the cats—Rudy was missing. The crying grew louder, coming from one of the small houses. I reach in and scooped Rudy up. He jerked and tossed in my arms, not to get down, but because he was having a seizure. I think he was totally unaware of me. I carefully placed him in a towel-lined box and began frantically calling our vet. Rudy fell into a deep sleep, only to wake again crying and jerking with seizures.

At the end of a twenty minute drive through the dark, Rudy lay motionless, barely breathing on a table in the vet's examination room; close up, his mouth and ears looked jaundiced. The doctor took urine and blood samples, and sadly shook his head. Rudy was dying, and neither the vet's skills, nor my hopes and prayers, could restore his physical health. A tiny needle inserted into a vein, and Rudy was gone in seconds.

Lab tests later revealed that Rudy had hepatic lipidosis, or fatty liver disease, and cardiomyopathy. If there had been early signs of his disease, Rudy was as adept at hiding them as he was at staying just out of reach.

I took Rudy's body home and buried it under a brilliantly blooming azalea bush. I miss Rudy, but I imagine his spirit is watching from a distance.

[This story was first published in *Cats & Kittens* magazine in November 2003.]

Sebastian
(1985-2003)
a story for Barbara

It was a hot summer afternoon when our cat, Sebastian, died. Sebastian had come to live at Sanctuary House when his former people could no long care for him. Now, he was old and thin and very ill. He went to sleep quietly, purring, then breathing deeply and slowly, until he was gone.

I prefer to remember him though, as the cat whom I had known before. Head and tail held high, Sebastian walked through his garden, in his wealthy Philadelphia suburb, into his cat door of his house. A large, orange tabby, he was the master of the garden, dignified and stately, but not above chasing a butterfly or another passing cat!

He had been adopted as a tiny foundling kitten in a rain storm into a college dorm; so, in fact, he was a well-educated, university cat.

When he came to live with us, his retirement arrangement, you might say, he enjoyed lazy afternoons, sunning on the steps, or curled up with a group of cat friends. He occasionally nodded to a passing butterfly, but seemed to cheer for the younger cats while they did the chasing. Sebastian loved other cats; he loved people; he even loved our barky cocker spaniel, Kelly.

Sebastian was always ecstatic when offered his favorite treat—a slice of American cheese—and was quite willing to sit patiently in front of the refrigerator until I realized what he wanted. He was always polite, but persistent, in asking to have doors opened for him. He didn't take himself or others too seriously, but he did know that he was a cat worthy of respect. Somehow, he imparted that feeling of self-worth to others as well; I was glad to open doors for Sebastian!

He was also ever the gentleman, allowing tiny Persian, Zella, to choose her nap space on the table or window sill, and to taste food from each dish and choose what she wanted, before he began to eat.

Sebastian was definitely a joy and delight!

Now, he is gone ahead, a little out of sight. Farewell, dear one. Farewell joyous one, delightful one—until we meet again on the other side.

Sofie

S he was, the first time I saw her, a magnificent flying cat. White magic, with a splash of black and gold, leaping through the tall grass, pouncing on a mouse. I presumed she was from one of the farms surrounding our rural neighborhood.

As summer turned to autumn, I would often see her in the early morning, hunting, and then disappearing into the tall grass and wild flowers in the next door field or under the abandoned building that used to be a country store. And then, I didn't see her for a long time. I missed her grace and vitality, but imagined that she had moved back into her home for the winter.

It was only when the snow covered our lawn and front steps that I discovered little cat feet leading up to the door and then away again. I left the barn door open slightly, with a dish of milk just inside. The next morning, the milk was gone. I left a can of cat food, and it too was eaten. One night at dusk, I went into the barn, and there she was, staring intently into the bales of hay. When she heard me, she leapt into the hay, and I suppose slipped out of the other side of the barn.

I wanted to bring her in, to be sure she had her shots, was spayed, and especially to know that she would have a warm, dry winter. It was easy to catch her in a Havahart trap. It was not easy to move her from the trap to a cat carrier—she escaped! "Wild," I thought, "I'll probably never see her again."

But no, she was back again the next day, eager for the canned food I had left out for her. I quietly stepped into the barn and shut the door. For the next two hours I talked and she watched me—from behind the lawn tractor, from the top of the hay bales, from the window sill, from behind the bicycles and other summer equipment stored in the corner. I tried to follow her, but of course, was no match for her! She could go under, over, and through things—she watched me stumble, knock things over, trip, and crash my way around the barn. At some point in our game, I started calling her Sofie. She looked at me and tilted her head to one side.

"Come on, Sofie," I pleaded as I held out a new can of tuna cat food. She sniffed and took a step toward me. Then, amazingly, she walked over and began eating out of the can. I hardly breathed. I reached out with my other hand, petted her head, and picked her up.

She was soft and gentle, not at all wild. But as I petted her, I felt her beginning-to-enlarge teats. "Oh, we're having kittens," I said to her. "Well, come on in."

I took Sofie to the vet for a rabies shot. "Are you going to have her spayed," I was asked. "What about the kittens?"

"Well, of course, she's going to be spayed," I answered, "eventually. We're having kittens first!" Judy, the vet tech, smiled at me. "That's what I'd do, too," she said, "but you never know. We have to ask."

"You don't have to ask me," I said. "I certainly wasn't planning to have kittens, but we are having kittens. And I'm sure I can find good homes for kittens."

Sofie moved into a guest bedroom. She ate, slept, grew bigger. She was fairly-well litter box trained, but kicked the litter with great gusto.

"Don't teach the kittens this trick," I told her every time I swept the floor.

Sofie was affectionate and unfazed by the barking of our dogs. She was most fond of curling up in the closet, so I made a special nesting space for her.

As it got nearer time for the kittens to be born, Sofie was very restless. And then, one morning, I heard a little mewing cry. I went in, and found Sofie cleaning one tiny, orange kitten. I knew one kitten wasn't all, but was not overly concerned when no other kittens appeared in the next several hours. Cats can temporarily stop or delay labor.

I left to teach a class at the nearby university. When

THE CATS OF SANCTUARY HOUSE

I got home, I went to check on Sofie. She was obviously in trouble. She still had the first kitten, but two others lay beside her—one deformed and still-born; the other, only barely alive. I picked up the gasping kitten, rubbed it and tried to clear its lungs, but it died in my hands. Sofie was breathing very hard. She suddenly shuddered and pushed—two more kittens, both dead.

"It's OK, Sofie," I whispered. "Take care of this one kitten." I wasn't sure if those were the last kittens or not. Sofie seemed exhausted; her eyes appeared glazed. And then came two more kittens—alive but having great difficulty breathing. Sofie looked at them and turned away. She lay down with her back to them. "Sofie, your babies," I pleaded. "You've got to help."

Frantically, I called Judy, "I don't know what to do," I admitted. "Swing them down, rub them—you've got to get them breathing and warm," she answered. "If Sofie can't help them, you'll have to."

Still panting, Sofie closed her eyes. I put the orange kitten against her stomach and began massaging the two little ones. The first, a little calico, made gurgling sounds, but gradually began breathing more evenly. The second, a tiny orange kitten, was cold, her paws bluish, but eventually she, too, seemed to move into life. I moved them close to their mother and opened their mouths around her protruding nipples.

By the next day, Sofie had recovered. She took excellent care of her kittens, but never allowed all three to be together. She left the first, a male, in the closet, but moved the two girls under the dresser. I made a towel nest for them, thinking Sofie would moved the three kittens under the dresser. But no, she made the trip between the two places, feeding the boy, and then the girls together.

Since Sofie, or Sophia, means "wisdom," and according to the Bible, wisdom is the mother of riches, we named the kittens Gold, Frankincense, and Myrrh—"Goldie," "Frankie," and "Mira."

At first, the kittens seemed to thrive, and I supposed that Sofie knew why she wanted to keep them in two places. Frankie was the loudest, always calling his mother while she was with the girls. Mira, who liked to drink lying on her back, grew much more quickly than Goldie. One of Mira's back legs turned under her, but I hoped it would grow stronger in time.

Then one morning when I went to check on the kittens, Frankie was dead. Sofie had wrapped him in the towel under the dresser and moved the girls back to the closet. I buried Frankie near the bodies of his brothers and sisters.

Mira and Goldie continue to grow into strong, playful kittens. They tumble and chase each other, and are beginning to ignore their mother's insistence that they come to her. Goldie is still smaller, but is the more adventurous of the two and also the one who likes to cuddle. Mira's weak leg has grown strong, and she is a strong climber and jumper. Their favorite toy is a roll of adding machine paper, unrolled of course, into a jumbled maze of fun!

Because of Sofie's difficult delivery and the death of so many kittens, we were afraid that she might be FELV/FIV positive; but no, she is healthy. The outlook for Goldie and Mira is excellent, too. In a few weeks, when Sofie's milk is dried up, it will be time to have her spayed.

And yes, Sofie, Goldie, and Mira, are staying right here, at home!

[This story was first published in *Cats & Kittens* magazine in July 2004.]

Solomon

The large, old, pale gold-colored cat was more than willing to enter the Havahart trap in exchange for a can of cat food. He had been out, living in the woods, on his own, for a very long time. A scar on his mouth and resulting crooked teeth were evidence that he had, on occasion, had to fight his way through life.

He was certainly a feral cat, but was remarkably passive. He would not at first, and will not now after months at Sanctuary House, allow himself to be picked up. But he loves to be petted, and if I sit on the floor, he will gladly climb into my lap to be held. He meows loudly to get my attention and head butts my legs until I reach down to him.

We named him Solomon, a name denoting wisdom, simply because a cat of his age would have to be wise to have lived in the wild and be in such relatively good health. And, like wise Solomon in the Bible, we were quite certain that this Solomon had fathered many, many children. After cat Solomon was neutered, he became even more affectionate, and I moved him to a room with several other cats. He, elderly Blossom, and Thomas II, have become fast friends. They are, after years of living a dangerous and difficult life outdoors on their own, enjoying the relative comforts of being "pets." They don't play with toys, but are obviously pleased by full food and water dishes, and a quiet, safe place to sleep.

However, Solomon's greatest claim to fame at Sanctuary House became evident only when Sofie's kittens were born. Although many of Sofie's seven kittens were stillborn or died shortly after birth, they were, except for two calicos, all a pale golden color. It stands to reason, and the time that we found Sofie and Solomon bears this out, that Solomon is the father of Sofie's kittens. Of course, the name Sofie also means Wisdom, so it's very logical that Solomon and Sofie go together!

The stamp of certainty on this relationship is Goldie, who looks every bit a miniature copy of Solomon! She is as much like Solomon as her sister, Mira, is like Sofie. And Goldie is, again like Solomon, very demanding of attention.

It wasn't planned, of course, but it is a source of much interest and amusement, watching the similarities on this little branch of a family tree.

Stormy

$\mathcal{T}$he end of the year had been strange—December was warm and balmy, with temperatures far above normal. And then, we were in a new year and there came a bitterly cold January. Sanctuary House is on the southern part of Maryland's Eastern Shore, and while the rest of the peninsula was whitened by a soft blanket of snow, we were pelted with freezing rain and sleet. Although the trees, bushes, tall grasses, fences, and electrical and telephone wires were rimed with ice that sparkled in the early morning light and clicked when the wind blew, the sky was a muted gray with the promise of more precipitation. The temperature was only 10 degrees, and with the wind chill, it felt like 10 degrees below zero.

Callie, our Arabian mare, whinnied to me as I walked carefully across the icy path to the garage/barn. "Just a few more weeks of this stormy weather," I reminded her. "You'll see—even February is going to be better."

I wanted to be outside for as short a time as possible—time to feed one horse, two goats, and flocks of Guineas, ducks, geese, and chickens. One side of the barn was piled high with bales of hay, a large drum held 300 pounds of whole corn, and I had recently bought 50 pound bags of horse and goat feed. In the house was a good supply of dog and cat food. Even if the storm lasted for a week or ten days, I would have no need to go out for feed.

The ducks began quacking ecstatically when they heard the corn clatter as I scooped it into a bucket, and a few mice scuttled past my feet, hoping some of the corn would drop down to them. I suddenly had the eerie feeling that I was being watched.

I looked up into the hay bales, and there nestled in a gap, was a gray cat. Actually, a long-haired, gray, white, black, and gold—calico cat. She regarded me with bright yellow eyes, and a guarded expression. "My goodness," I said to her, "you are a stormy weather cat!"

She stayed snug in the hay while I fed the other animals, and then quickly devoured a can of cat food that I took to her. I closed the barn door, wanting her to stay warm and dry. At this point, there was no possibility of a visit to the vet, and I did not want to introduce a strange cat to my other cats. I felt certain that this cat must have a home nearby, because she was not thin, and she certainly was tame.

I called a nearby neighbor who has a gray cat. "No," she replied, "my cat is right here, inside."

The county humane society and I contacted local veterinarians and other animal shelters. No one came forward to claim the storm cat.

"Okay, I think you live here now," I said to her, "and I think your name must be Stormy." Stormy reached out a paw to touch my hand, and slowly she began to purr.

By early the following week, the weather had cleared

and I took Stormy for a check up. Her tests were all negative. She was vaccinated and spayed.

For a new cat, moving into a large established group of cats can be a daunting experience. Stormy was certainly not an aggressor—in fact, she hid under the bed. And then, slowly, she began to interact with the other cats; eventually, she moved on to the bed itself, sharing a blanket with Ragu and Quin. I believe she knows that now she is loved and wanted.

And I, who love warm weather and sunshine? Even I would have to agree: some wonderful surprises can come with ice storms!

Theo

The third cat at Sanctuary House—well, before there even was an official Sanctuary House—was Theo.

Theo was found as a tiny, less-than-one-week-old kitten behind a small restaurant in a popular tourist area. The kitten's eyes were still tightly closed and his ears lay folded close to his head.

The man who found the kitten took him to a local veterinarian who then called me. I was thrilled to have Theo at our house and, I think, even Thomas and Gussie, the original two cats, welcomed him as well. Molly, the golden retriever, had never seen such a small kitten and watched in complete fascination as I fed and cared for the bright orange little creature.

Several days after he came home, the kitten opened his eyes. He snuggled into the crook of my arm and we became instant friends. I definitely wanted this kitten to be a "Canterbury Tail,"—named after an Archbishop of Canterbury—and to find the perfect name, I read slowly aloud a list of the Archbishops of Canterbury. At that time there were 103 names on the list, and the first time through, the kitten didn't move or make a sound.

I began reading the list again... number seven on the list was Theodorus, who became Archbishop of Canterbury in 668. When I read his name, the kitten yawned and stretched his small paw toward my face.

"So that's who you are," I said to him. I looked at him carefully. "You don't look like a 'Ted' or 'Teddy'," I continued, "you must be 'Theo'."

As a small kitten, Theo was affectionate and easygoing. He liked to be held and even initiated games with the other cats and with me. But, as he grew into a gangly adolescent, his personality changed. He became extremely shy and fearful.

The first time I noticed this was one day when I had come in from cutting the grass. Theo ran from me and hid behind a chair; he hissed when I tried to pick him up. I assumed that he did not like the odor of the grass clippings that were stuck to my shoes, but even when I had showered and changed clothes, Theo would not come to me.

Then Theo stopped playing with the other cats, and although he played with toys on his own, he never included me in his games either. If the older cats and I tried to play with him, he stopped immediately and walked or ran away. Theo seemed to be entirely in his own world; he responded to me with growls and hisses, or not at all.

I took Theo for a veterinary check-up, but no physical problems were found. I was afraid that I had done something harmful as I raised him, but the vet assured me that was not the case—some cats, he said, are just like this. Perhaps, not having a cat mother, Theo missed some crucial learning component in his trip to feline adulthood; or perhaps genetically, Theo is not a particularly friendly cat.

Today, Theo lives in our cat courtyard. He has a few special cat friends: Sasha, Tip, Patrick, and Gracie. And he occasionally interacts with the rest of us! We just allow Theo to be himself and, I think, he has taught us to be more tolerant and accepting of others... a good mission in life, even for a cat!

Thomas
(1984-2001)

The vet and I agreed— no "heroic" measures. Thomas was, at the age of seventeen, dying—probably of congestive heart failure. He had been slowing down noticeably for the past several months, leaving his favorite rocking chair only at meal times and for trips to the litter box. Occasionally, he ventured upstairs and then stood, waiting patiently, to be lifted onto my bed.

"We could try antibiotics," the vet offered. It was late on a Friday.

"Okay," I said, "but nothing invasive. I do not want to cause him any pain."

And so, we went home. I tried to make Thomas as

comfortable as possible. He quickly fell asleep in his rocking chair.

On Saturday morning, he followed Gussie, his long-time companion, to the kitchen—a good sign, I assumed. But he only looked at the dish of food, and turned away. He spent most of the day curled in a chair; Gussie curled beside him, with her head resting on his shoulder.

Later, in the afternoon, I held him and rocked him. Gussie stayed nearby. In fact, she had not left him all day.

Gussie ate supper. Thomas watched her. He drank a little water and a teaspoon of tuna fish juice.

Then, suddenly, he turned and fell. He was dead. Gussie gazed at him, sniffed at his face, then stepped over his body. In death, cats are uncomplicated. Gussie knew. Thomas was there; now Thomas was not there.

On Sunday morning, very early, at sunrise, I prepared to bury Thomas in an old, historic, church graveyard.

"Don't you have to ask first?" Sister Harriet queried.

"Oh, they'd probably have to have a vestry meeting," I responded. "I don't think we can wait that long, and anyway, you know it's easier to get forgiveness than permission. Don't worry," I promised. "I'll let them know I did it."

It was the Sunday before Christmas, but fortunately the ground was not frozen. I dug a hole away from the human graves, near a bend in the river bordering the cemetery. There were geese on the water. Thomas would like this spot, I thought.

I hadn't expected to see anyone, but an elderly woman was putting a wreath on a nearby grave. We looked at each other in the thin early morning light. Both of us had tears in our eyes—maybe from the cold. "It's a beautiful place, isn't it?" I was glad she had spoken first. "My husband has been here eleven years."

"I just buried my cat," I offered. "Do you think your husband would mind?"

"Oh, he'd love having a cat near," she said.

I went back for the eleven A.M. service. At the

door, the priest asked, "Did you know there are some famous people buried in our graveyard—a former governor, an actress, a spy."

"Well, the most famous one buried here is my cat," I said. I considered that I had told him about the burial.

Several weeks later, I took our rambunctious puppy for a walk in the graveyard. Exercise for her, a visit to Thomas' grave for me.

The grave had been torn open. The place where I had left Thomas was empty.

My first reaction was guilt. I should have dug the hole deeper. I should have put rocks on top. I should have made the grave next to a human one, beside the caretaker's building, nearer the church.

And then I had a more rational thought. Perhaps it is more honorable to be devoured by a wild animal than to be eaten by worms and bacteria. I thought Thomas would have agreed with that.

Only later, for the first time in my life, did I realize that I could understand and empathize with people who doubt the Resurrection. The grave was empty.

There was no body. Somebody had taken the body away. That's much easier to believe than resurrection!

I know Thomas didn't rise from the dead. His cat spirit though—well, it's alive and well, aiding my understanding, keeping me empathetic.

[This story was first published in *Cats & Kittens* magazine in January 2004.]

Thomas II
a story for Jim

*A*fter Abbie's injuries had healed and her kittens were born, the vet laughed as he looked at the kittens. "And who is your father?" he had asked. The one thing that all five kittens had in common were tiger stripes: the calico, an orange, and three grays, each with a distinctive striped pattern.

Their father? We believe—ninety-nine percent sure—he is Thomas II. Although at first, the connection between Abbie and Thomas II was a mystery.

Not long after Abbie came to Sanctuary House, while she was still recovering from the emergency surgery that removed her lower jaw that had been nearly shot off, and before we knew that she was pregnant, a gray striped cat came through the tall weeds of the goat pasture.

A strong, relatively healthy-looking male, the cat had an infected injury on his left front leg and was wildly feral. The cat was hungry and slipped easily into a carrier in exchange for a can of turkey dinner cat food. I took him to the vet where he was neutered and his wound treated. The wound, we concluded, was caused by shot from a pellet gun—the same kind of gun that had injured Abbie.

I had planned to release the cat back into the woods behind Sanctuary House, but there was that wound! He had to continue antibiotics for a week, so he would have to stay in. I named him Thomas II, in memory of my first cat, Thomas, and in the hope that being named for such a gentle cat would help tame this wild one. "Thomas II" was quickly shortened to "T2" or "Tom Two."

T2 had no intention of quietly settling into being a house cat! I had made a space for him in a large crate, but the first time I opened the door to clean the litter box, he jumped out. He ran through the living room, behind the piano, into the kitchen, across the kitchen counters, and finally into the pantry. Fortunately, the pantry is a large, walk-in one, with light and a glass window in the door.

Unfortunately, I was not planning on having a cat live there, and had stored paper goods, light bulbs, and other household items in the back of the long, narrow room! T2 snuggled right in between two packages of paper towels. I carefully, gradually, rearranged the pantry to make room for a litter box and cat dishes. For the next week, the pantry was T2's home.

As often as possible, I went into the pantry to talk with T2 and get him used to my presence. At the end of the week, his medicine finished, T2 patiently climbed into a cat carrier. I took him upstairs, where he joined a small group of other cats. T2 is still extremely shy, although he does, on occasion, allow me to pet him; he is gentle and affectionate with the other cats.

Not long ago, Abbie's kittens were born. Not only

do they have T2's same striped pattern, but one of them, Linus, looks exactly like T2—they even have the identical white and gray markings on their stomachs, and they have golden eyes!

As closely as we can tell, Abbie and Thomas II were probably caterwauling through the night when someone shot them both. The pellets that shot across Abbie's face would have been at exactly the right level to hit T2's front leg.

When the kittens were old enough, and Abbie had been spayed, I put her temporarily in the room with T2 and his group of cats. I don't know if they remembered each other, but I did once find them sitting side by side on a book case, looking for all the world as if they were posing for a family portrait.

Abbie has moved to the cat courtyard, where she is the alpha calico! T2 is staying indoors for now. And the kittens... well, their stories are for the future!

Tiger

Tiger had been taken to the vet by his owner. The senior cat was no longer eating, and since he was already thin, his owner feared the worst. A quick check revealed what appeared to be throat cancer. Tiger's owner at first agreed to a biopsy, but then decided to have the elderly cat euthanized, and said his last good-byes.

However, with the biopsy on its way to the lab, the vet decided to try antibiotics in the meantime. Amazingly, Tiger began to get better! The mass in his throat shrank and he began to eat and drink. It seemed that Tiger had a good chance for recovery.

"That's great," I said to Susan. "So he can go home?"

"Yes," she replied. "We're going to keep him here

for a few more days, but he's really doing better than anyone could have imagined!"

Early the following week she called me. "You can take Tiger the next time you're here. He's ready to go home."

"Home? Home with me?" I was completely surprised. "I thought he was going to his own home."

"No," she said. "His owner is moving and didn't think he would survive the confusion. He's yours."

And that's how Tiger came to live at Sanctuary House!

At the clinic, Tiger had been passive and mellow, an easy-going cat who was aloof, but quietly friendly. At Sanctuary House he was—well, a tiger! He had been a predominantly outdoor cat in his previous home, and he let me know right away that he had no intention of staying in the house. He moved to the courtyard, but was not so sure that he wanted many cat friends. I tried to pick him up and he screeched and fought to get down. If I ignored him, he called out for attention. Happily, tuna cat food cures many frustrations! Tiger ate a whole can of tuna and settled down. He found a favorite spot to sleep between the brick steps and an overgrown mint plant.

Because he is an old cat, I encouraged him to come inside on a recent very hot day. He stepped into the house, looked around, and roared in his best tiger voice, "No, this isn't the right place for me either!"

But now, we have discovered an arrangement that makes us both happy. Tiger has his own cat condo, complete with shelves for climbing, where he spends most of his time. He demands and receives canned cat food for breakfast, and has a window full of sunlight for extended cat-napping. He is content as the king of his now private domain!

And his throat problem—which was not cancer after all—is a thing of the past.

Tiger has come home—oh, yes!

Tip and Sasha

Tip and Sasha were the first kittens actually born at Sanctuary House. Their mother, a tabby cat I had never seen, and who was apparently on her way somewhere else, gave birth to five kittens in rapid succession, right in the driveway on the hottest-ever July 4th! She took a black and white kitten and disappeared under a nearby building.

I moved the other kittens to the shade of the porch, expecting her to return—but soon enough, I discovered that they were mine alone. Two of the kittens died in the first three days: a very tiny gray one and a tabby. Both sucked with difficulty and never really grew. The two other kittens, both tabbies, grew and were soon adding a measure of excitement to our otherwise calm household.

As a wildlife rehabilitator, I happened to have several ducklings living in the dining room while the kittens were still quite small. Every night, I carefully put everyone to bed, so imagine my surprise one morning to find kittens and ducklings parading around the room! One precocious duckling seemed to be the leader as ducklings and kittens followed him under chairs, across the Oriental rug, and over a stack of books.

The kittens, of course, needed names. In keeping with our custom of naming the cats after Archbishops of Canterbury, we named the girl, Michaela—for Archbishop Michael Ramsey; and the boy, Anselm—after St. Anselm, a name dating back to the days of single names. The kittens, however, thought of themselves by different names. Michaela has white feet and a tiny white tip on her tail. "You should call her Tip," my friend Meg commented, and the name stuck.

I did try calling the other kitten Anselm, but he never paid any attention. And every time I looked at him or picked him up, I seemed to hear him say, "My name is Alexander—for the Russian theologian Alexander Schmemann." I couldn't imagine how a kitten could dream up that name—I have been a Sister for a very long time, and had once lived near St. Vladimir's Seminary in New York City, where I had often heard of Alexander Schmemann. But even I had never read any of his books... I wondered how this kitten knew about him! Finally, I gave in. "Okay, okay, Alexander Anselm," I said, "and I'll call you a nickname for Alexander—Sasha."

Sasha and Tip are thin cats, and Sasha is especially long and slinky. They are easy-going and the other cats enjoy being with them. As a young kitten, Sasha was a caretaker for Tip. He stayed close to her and never let other cats play roughly with her. But as they grew older, Tip became the leader of the two, initiating cat games and being the first one to venture into new situations. Tip jumps out at other cats from a hiding place under a chair or behind a table leg, and she is the one who makes toys from a leaf, a feather, or even a slip of paper.

I never realized how dependent on each other Tip and Sasha are until they were apart for a few days. We were moving houses and took Tip in the first cat transport. The other cats were arriving over the next two weeks. We were going back and forth between both houses, insuring that everyone had adequate and proper care. But it was not long—only a day or two—before Sasha became very ill. He was completely limp and refused to eat. Blood tests and a thorough examination revealed no physical problems.

"Get him back with his sister," the vet advised. When Tip and Sasha were reunited, he recovered almost immediately, miraculously.

"You'd better always keep them together," the vet said on a follow-up visit, and on Sasha's record card noted, "Totally attached to sibling!"

Today Tip and Sasha live in the courtyard at Sanctuary House. Each has special friends. Sasha likes to lounge around with Theo, Henry, Gracie, Patrick, and Nori; Tip likes to run and play with Moses, Caroline, Lucie, Ari, and Zoë. They are often in different areas: Sasha in the cat house; Tip under the blue and white sun umbrella.

But from the corner of their eyes, they are always watching each other, paying attention in that I-don't-see-you way of watching that typifies all cats, a perfect example of pure, sibling affection.

Tut

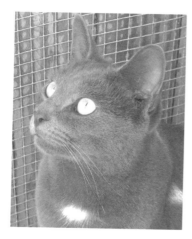

The skinny gray cat walked slowly around from behind the aviary building at Sanctuary House. Unlike most cats who just turn up, this one was tame and friendly, and meowed to be picked up. When I did pick him up, he wrapped his legs around my arm and began to climb toward my head.

"Whoa, little guy," I said. "I don't even know who you are."

The little Siamese mix cat stared at me. "Please, please, keep me," he seemed to beg. He was one cat with hundreds of ticks and fleas. I treated the fleas and ticks, and found a can of cat food.

"Who are you," I asked the now much happier cat.

"Tutankhamen," he answered, "but I bet you can't even spell that! Just call me Tut."

Tut was young, but old enough to make kittens. One trip to the vet later, and Tut was not only declared healthy, but also was neutered. We came home, and after two days, Tut moved to the cat courtyard. In spite of being the young, new guy, he made friends with the other cats quite easily. Affectionate Tut found cats with similar personalities, especially Henry, Sully, Mira, and Zoë, and they were soon playing together as though they had always known each other.

And then, two months later, Tut began to show signs that all might not be well. He lost a lot of fur around his neck and face. I was afraid that he might have ringworm—fortunately, that test was negative. We switched to a special food in case he had an allergy. Tut didn't like the allergy food, and insisted on eating what every other cat had. In a few weeks, though, his fur was back, thick and soft.

Just when I thought everything was fine with him, Tut suddenly got very sick. He had lost a little weight, but that was not uncommon considering the summer heat; but then he stopped eating altogether. His gums were almost white, and the back of his mouth was jaundiced. I tried putting food in his mouth, afraid that I would lose a second cat, as I had lost Rudy, to liver disease, but he began vomiting. I lifted Tut into a carrier and took him to the vet.

The vet looked in Tut's mouth and listened to his heart and breathing. "This is the sickest cat you've ever brought to me," he said. The problem was, he believed a flea borne disease.

"But he doesn't have fleas," I protested.

"Well, he did when you found him," he continued, "and the disease has been dormant until now. I almost never see this disease anymore. I'll draw blood for tests; we'll know for sure tomorrow, but we'll begin treatment today. There is not time to lose. You'll have to leave him here for a few days."

"Will he be alright?" I asked.

"I don't know," he answered.

I called the next morning. The first tests were negative. "I guess I was wrong," the vet said honestly. "Now I really don't know what he has, but we'll get more test results this afternoon."

In the meantime, Tut had begun to eat on his own and the food was staying down.

Later in the afternoon, I called again. "The tests were positive," the vet said. "We're treating him for the right thing."

Our vet is an excellent diagnostician—I would have trusted his observations over a simple lab test, but it was nice to know that science had confirmed his opinion! "It's good that you came when you did," the vet explained. "Without help and the right medication, Tut would have been dead within 48 hours."

Tut is home now, and has regained almost all of his lost weight. I wonder if all along Tut knew that he was sick—maybe when he begged, "Please, please keep me," he knew that he would need help to survive.

"Always listen to your vet," Tut said, "and always listen to your cat, too!"

Woollie and Zella-Judy

I was surprised one day to discover that Pearl, an elderly woman I had often visited in her retirement village townhouse, had been moved to a nursing home in another part of the state. I had promised Pearl that I would take care of her long-haired cat, Duchess, and I could not find Pearl or Duchess. Eventually I learned that Pearl's family had requested that no follow-up information be given out. I decided to search for Duchess. I contacted local veterinarians, animal shelters, and the county humane society.

For one breathless moment, I thought I had found Duchess in a small cage at the humane society. A long-haired gray cat lay pressed against the glass.

"No," the attendant replied, "that cat was brought in by her owners who no longer wanted her when they had a baby. She's an older cat, almost nine, and she doesn't have much time left. Her name is Woollie."

I was determined not to look at the cat, but as the attendant and I spoke the cat turned to look at me. The fur on her back was thin and flat from having been pressed against the glass. "Get me out of here," she seemed to say.

I hesitated. I already had many cats at home, but I would have taken Duchess, so another cat was not out of the question. I had now been looking for Duchess for weeks and I no longer expected to find her.

"I think I'll take Woollie home," I said to the attendant. "She looks like she needs a new home."

I signed papers and promised to take Woollie to my vet. She was already spayed and was up-to-date on her shots, so this would just be a routine check up.

"If you like older cats," the attendant added as I prepared to leave, "we have another old Persian. Actually someone is coming to look at her today, but if they don't want her, her time is up. Her name is Sassy, because she looks just like the cat in *Homeward Bound*. She was found as a stray, but she is spayed and declawed."

"Well, let me know," I responded. I felt sure that the people coming to see the Persian would want her. After all, Sassy in the movie was a very cute cat!

Woollie was not at all happy to find herself in a multiple cat household, but little by little she began to warm to the other cats. She and Nori, the other long-haired gray cat who lives at Sanctuary House, at first hissed and circled each other and then agreed to ignore each other. Woollie and Theo, a very large orange cat, settled on the same arrangement. With other cats, however, Woollie established more positive friendships—Woollie, Ruby and Maggie enjoy cat naps in the sun, sitting together but making no demands on each other. Woollie has grown into an elegant cat—aloof, but self-assured and content.

A few weeks after Woollie came home, and just about the time she was settling in, the humane society called.

"You'll have to come today, if you want her—Sassy, I mean," the caller said in a somewhat hushed voice.

I went to sign for Sassy as soon as I could. Humane society Sassy does in fact look like movie Sassy. She is tiny, thin and intensely determined. "You have to bring her back if you don't want her," the attendant said.

"We won't be back," I replied.

I took Sassy home. If Woollie had been annoyed by discovering that she has many brother and sister cats, Sassy was even more exasperated. She did not respond to the name Sassy at all, so I gave her a new name, Zella. I hoped that with love and affection, she too would become a more social cat. Little by little, Zella began acknowledging her new name. Surely, I thought, she would become more outgoing, perhaps even jump into my lap or chase another cat, or play with a catnip mouse.

But, if the truth is told, Zella prefers to sit quietly by herself. She enjoys human attention for several minutes each day, but does not ordinarily enjoy feline attention at all! She is content to find her own special spot in a room—sometimes on a chair or behind a book case, or on top of a pile of papers.

Zella's most common response to unwanted attention is to ignore the entire situation, so I was not surprised that on a visit to the vet she sat unmoving on the examination table with her eyes tightly closed. I talked softly to her, trying to elicit some reaction. The veterinarian's assistant came in to fill in details on Zella's chart.

"Judy," someone called to the assistant from the next room. Suddenly Zella sat up and opened her eyes wide.

"Judy?" I whispered to her. She turned toward me and stared into my face.

"I am Judy," she thought, "you may call me Zella or you may call me Judy—and sometimes, when I want to, I will answer you!"

Zella-Judy has found a favorite quiet place, behind a chair, near a window. And sometimes she does let me into the tiny corner of her world.

Afterword

Ernest Hemingway said it best, "One cat just leads to another." That has been my experience: Thomas led to Augusta, to Theo, Tip and Sasha. And so it continues!

Since I wrote this book, several changes have taken place in the Sanctuary House "catdom"—that area ruled by felines.

Young, exotic-looking Tut died suddenly, unexpectedly of cardiomyopathy.

Gentle Casey died of inoperable throat cancer.

Aaron died of kidney failure. After he was diagnosed I changed his diet to a prescription food, but he did not rally for long. With his increasing weakness, Ari wanted to be with his cat friends and shunned any attention from me. He curled up with Nori, Leo, or Tovia, or sat close to his brother Moses. The day before he died, Solomon lay close to him keeping him warm, offering cat wisdom and comfort. Finally, Ari allowed me to rub his head and ears and stroke his bony back. I hoped he would let me hold him. I reached to pick him up—he calmly turned to look at me and then raised his right paw. I knew he meant, "No, you may not pick me up!" I blew him a kiss. The next morning, I held his lifeless body close to my heart before I buried it in the garden.

My darling Annie died of lung cancer. Some people believe that animals cross a rainbow bridge when they die. I don't know about that detail, but I do believe they are reunited in heaven with the people they have loved here. "Run, find Ron," I whispered to Annie, as she gently breathed out of this life and into the next.

Tiny, gray, foundling Lydia, died of fading kitten syndrome; and three rescues from a late-term cat spay, William, Winston, and Lily, had only a glimmer of a chance, and died within a week.

But it has not been all loss!

First came a middle-aged, heavy-set gray cat, whose person had died. In the past she had been affectionately called "Trash" by some, and "Sweetie" by others.

I combined the names and call her Stash because she is very valuable to me.

Black and white, eighteen-year-old Chincoteague, named after the island where she was born, came when her person moved to Sweden. Our multi-cat situation was a challenge, but Chinc gradually warmed to her new home. She tolerates the young kittens' antics, treating Ida, Ada, and Dora almost as her own. Meeting our elderly spitz, Minnie, was a surprise, but Chinc rose to the occasion. She swatted the little dog between the eyes, catching a paw full of fur, pulling Minnie toward her. Minnie yelped and immediately lay down. Ever since she has regarded Chinc with casual indifference, proving that cats can teach old dogs new tricks!

Our most recent feline addition is Chloe, a small tabby cat, whose person, because of illness, could no longer care for her. At age eleven, she is learning the intricacies of living with many other cats and becoming friends with Rosie, Quin, and Goldie.

What a legacy my Thomas left... one cat does indeed lead to another!

The Cats of Sanctuary House